Disney
Z·O·M·B·I·E·S

Copyright © 2018 Disney Enterprises, Inc. All rights reserved. Published in the
United States by Random House Children's Books, a division of Penguin Random
House LLC, 1745 Broadway, New York, NY 10019, and in Canada by Penguin
Random House Canada Limited, Toronto, in conjunction with Disney Enterprises,
Inc. Random House and the colophon are registered trademarks of Penguin
Random House LLC.

rhcbooks.com

ISBN 978-0-7364-3963-3

Printed in the United States of America

10 9 8 7 6 5 4 3 2 1

The Junior Novelization

Adapted by Judy Katschke
Based on *Zombies*, written by David Light and Joseph Raso

Random House  New York

CHAPTER 1

With a head of electric-green hair, chalky skin, and red-rimmed eyes, fifteen-year-old Zed was drop-dead gorgeous. He was also a zombie, about to attend Seabrook High—his first human school ever!

"There's no one more excited about today than me!" Zed told himself as he got ready for school. On his first day at Seabrook, he would wear what all zombies would be wearing for the rest of their lives: regulation coveralls and a Z-Band.

The Z-Band delivered soothing electromagnetic pulses that kept zombies from munching on brains and faces. To zombies, brains and faces had once been finger-eating good, but not anymore. Now, finally, fifty years after the zombie outbreak, humans could be near a zombie without worrying—too much!

Not wanting to be late for his first day, Zed headed downstairs. On the way to the kitchen, he passed a wall covered with framed family photos. In most of them, his little sister, Zoey, held Zander, her much-loved stuffed puppy. Zed was shown holding his favorite item—a football.

Zed's plan was to try out for the high school football team, the Mighty Shrimp, and become the school's first zombie player. At Seabrook High, with their pep rallies and cheerleading competitions, cheerleaders ruled. Zed hoped to make Seabrook's football team as successful as their cheer squad!

Stepping into the kitchen, Zed saw Zoey clutching her stuffed puppy. Humans still believed zombies would eat pets, so they were not allowed to own any. For now, only stuffed animals and deady bears would do. Or big brothers pretending to be pets to make their little sisters happy. . . .

Dropping to his hands and knees, Zed padded across the kitchen toward Zoey. He tilted his head, flashed puppy-dog eyes, and barked. "Woof!"

Zoey giggled. Her brother's impression of a puppy

was always dead-on. "Good boy!" she cooed. "Good boy!"

Zed's puppy act was interrupted by his dad, Zevon, carrying a platter over from the stove. Zevon knew the importance of a good breakfast, especially on the first day of school.

"Try this, son," Zevon said, proudly presenting his latest mush-terpiece. "Brains in a can!"

Zed raised an eyebrow. Wait a minute—did he say brains?

"It's made of cauliflower," Zevon added quickly.

Zed took a bite and wrinkled his nose. "It tastes like gym sneakers, Dad," he said.

"I know!" Zevon said excitedly. "How great is that?"

Zevon placed the family-size platter on the table, and they all dug in. Zed tossed his football up and down as he ate. Zevon sighed.

"Zed, I don't know about this football thing," his dad admitted. "It might be too much."

"What do you mean?" Zed asked, still eating.

"You're great, but you've had very little contact with humans," Zevon explained. "And humans don't like zombies."

Zed looked up from his plate and smiled. "That's

because they haven't met me yet!"

Zevon smiled too. There was no stopping his son, especially when it came to football. He just hoped the human kids wouldn't be too much of an obstacle.

Little sis Zoey wasn't worried about her brother. She offered him a stuffed dog bone and said, "Who's a good boy?"

"Me!" Zed exclaimed before snatching the bone between his teeth.

Though he joined in the playful tug-of-war, Zed knew a zombie's life wasn't all games. They had curfews every night, and their coveralls were anything but glam. But Zed was a die-hard optimist. For the first time ever, zom-kids would go to a human school, and he would try out for the football team. And that was progress!

No doubt, Zed was super-stoked about his first day at Seabrook High. But on the other side of the tracks in the pristinely perfect human town of Seabrook, someone was just as excited and, as always, had a lot to cheer about!

CHAPTER 2

"Gimme an F! Gimme an I! Gimme an R-S-T!"

Fifteen-year-old Addison cheered dynamically as she performed splits and cartwheels through her pastel-colored room. Her walls were plastered with cheerleading pennants and pom-poms. The pom-poms seemed to shake on their own as she shouted, "It's the first day of freshman year for me! Me! Me!"

Addison stopped in front of her full-length mirror to check out her hair and spirit. Ever since she was a little kid, she had crushed cheer summer camp year after year. But today she would crush the tryouts for the Seabrook High cheer squad!

"You make cheer and you fit in!" Addison told her reflection. And why wouldn't she fit in? Her cheers were awesome, and she was a totally normal teen. A totally normal teen with a secret. . . .

Addison glanced over her shoulder to make sure the coast was clear. She then pulled a shimmery, silvery strand of hair from beneath her long blond wig. She never knew where the weird hair had come from. She just knew she was born with it, and nothing, not even serious hair dye, would cover it up.

Maybe in some places Addison's silvery hair would be cool, but not in Seabrook. Here, everyone dressed pretty much the same, and they all lived in identical houses. The people of Seabrook hated anything different and were proud of it.

That was why Addison had worn a wig for as long as she could remember. If anyone, besides her family, found out she had silver hair, she would lose friends and the thing she loved most—cheerleading!

Addison sighed, tucking her top-secret hair back underneath her wig. She gave her reflection one last look and then joined her parents downstairs.

Her dad, Dale, was chief Zombie Patrol officer and

had the shiny badge to prove it. Her mom, Missy, was mayor of Seabrook and an all-around big cheese.

When Dale and Missy saw Addison, they beamed with pride.

"Cheer tryouts today!" Missy declared.

"Cheer tryouts today!" Dale echoed.

Addison pumped the air with her fist and said, "Yes! Woo! I'm way fired up!"

"Seabrook has won every cheer championship since forever," Missy pointed out.

"Forever," Dale agreed.

"And now," Missy sighed, "with city council allowing zombies in our schools, we need cheer even more."

Missy looked Addison straight in the eye. "As mayor, I beseech you," she said. "Make that team! Win that championship!"

Addison wanted to roll her eyes. Beseech? Seriously?

"Nothing is going to stop you, Addison!" Dale said.

"As long as you keep that wig on," Missy reminded her.

Addison nodded. Her mom and dad didn't have a

thing to worry about. She was full of pep and oozing with normalcy. What more could Seabrook parents want?

"Go, team!" Addison cheered.

Dale and Missy waved from the doorstep as Addison headed down the street. Addison waved back to her parents and then to everyone she passed—the businessmen carrying identical briefcases marching off to work, a perfectly groomed mom pushing a shiny baby carriage, a trio of kids riding matching gleaming brand-new bicycles. Every house was a picture of pastel-painted perfection. Seabrook was decidedly normal.

Swinging her pom-poms and smiling from ear to ear, Addison headed for her new school. As long as she kept her real hair a secret, what could go wrong? After all, cheering was in her family genes, and her whole family was counting on her. No pressure.

Like a flawless cheer routine, Addison fell in with her friends and cousin Bucky on the seaside promenade. The crowd went wild as Bucky backflipped his way down the boardwalk. He wasn't just head cheerleader at Seabrook High—he was Seabrook's cheer rock star!

Bucky stopped flipping to hold up his hand. "No more autographs," he told the adoring fans.

He was soon joined by cheerleaders Stacey, Lacey, and Tracey. Next to Bucky, the Aceys were cheerleading royalty.

Addison hurried to keep up with Bucky and the Aceys as they sashayed down the promenade toward school. Their similar clothes were the colors of ice cream, their expressions cool as ice.

"Today's the day," Bucky said, "Are you ready, Cuz?"

Addison nodded excitedly. Ready? Seriously? All summer long, the first thing on her mind was making the Seabrook High cheerleading squad.

And the last thing on her mind was zombies!

CHAPTER 3

Stepping out his front door, Zed looked down the street. Things in Zombietown were worn and shabby but still very much alive.

Zed waved to his neighbors as he headed to school. Zombie workers wearing matching coveralls waved back. So did the zombie mom pushing a carriage constructed lovingly from scraps of wood and metal. The zombie kids riding unique double-decker bicycles would have waved too, had they not been gripping their handlebars.

Zed smiled. Who said Zombietown was a dead-end place? He stopped to study a wilting bloom in a flower box. Maybe it just needed a little water? He grabbed a nearby hose and turned it on. Instead of water, the hose spewed dust. He shook it again and again until a few drops of water came out. Success!

Zed continued on his way. Zombie kids seemed to pour from doors as he walked past haggard-looking houses. Their back-to-school clothes were government-issued zombie coveralls, but the students styled them to the max with repurposed objects—anything to show off their individuality.

Zed stopped at a house covered with anti-zombie graffiti. He knocked on the door, and Eliza stepped out. Eliza didn't see things the way Zed did. She believed that zombies would never be accepted by humans and that they needed to rise up.

Eliza dreamed of starting a zombie revolution. In the meantime, she was a tech geek with an amazing knowledge of code!

Zed and Eliza walked a few blocks before seeing their friend Bonzo busily painting a mural. A master artist, Bonzo could paint like Picasso. He also gave hugs like a bear!

When Bonzo wasn't expressing himself through art or hugs, he was expressing himself through Zombie speak: *"A zig, zagg, gwag, gwad, ziggy, got, gon, ziggity, got, goat, zag, ziggy, got, zong!"*

Zed and his friends scaled the wall that separated their street from the Seabrook Energy Plant. They landed in rubble, kicked up some dust, and then raced to an ancient fence by the barrier wall between Zombietown and Seabrook. Marching through a hole in the fence, they headed toward school.

For Zed, change had finally come. He and his zombuds were going to a real school with real human kids. No longer would they have to sit through classes in a dark, damp zombie basement. Their new classrooms would be bright, airy, and totally high-tech!

But when Zed, Eliza, and Bonzo reached Seabrook High, they weren't greeted by welcoming teachers or students. Instead, they were greeted by a tall fence that split the front entrance. On one side of the school entrance was a sign that read ZOMBIES. On the other side was one that read NORMALS.

"Enjoy the view, monsters!" Bucky sneered from the other side of the fence.

Eliza scowled, but Bonzo smiled—and howled through the fence straight at Bucky.

When Bucky saw the hulking zombie, he howled too. "Aiiiieeeeee!" He then took a breath, collected himself, and muttered, "Whatever."

The Zombie Patrol guard was not as dismissing. She marched up to Bonzo and narrowed her eyes. "Do we need to take a trip downtown?" she demanded.

"No, Officer," Zed piped up quickly.

"*Hagrazug?*" Bonzo asked.

"No, Bonzo, she doesn't want a hug," Zed murmured.

The Zombie Patrol guard gave Zed, Eliza, and Bonzo one last lingering glare. She then made sure all the zom-kids left the human students alone as they filed into the school.

Zed looked through the fence at his human classmates. Only one, Addison, looked back.

Who is she? Zed wondered.

As the human students walked up the stairs to the main entrance, Bucky looked over his shoulder at Addison. "We can't let those monsters change this town, Cuz," he insisted. "Ewwww!"

Addison frowned. Her family hated zombies, bigtime. But she didn't. Not really. "They're just going to school like us," she told Bucky.

Bucky froze on the steps to glare at Addison. Did he just hear what he thought he heard?

"Like us?" Bucky squealed. "People love me. I've got jazz hands. Those freaks are nothing like us,

Addison—they ate our grandfather!"

"It was just a small bite," Addison said.

Bucky drew in a deep breath. Small bite? Really? Sometimes he couldn't believe they shared DNA!

At the top of the steps, Bucky stopped to sign a few autographs and make an announcement: "Cheer tryouts after school, everybody. Let's go, Mighty Shrimp!"

The adoring crowd oohed and aahed as Bucky cartwheeled off, leaving Addison with another aspiring cheerleader, named Bree.

Bree had glasses and wore a huge smile as she babbled to Addison. "I always dreamed of being on cheer squad because I want to be a flier tossed high in the sky. People call me Bubbly Bree. Sometimes they say Babbly Bree, but I don't know why." Addison smiled as Bree tapped her forehead and cried, "Woo! Head rush!"

"Nice to meet you, Bree," Addison said. "I'm Addison. I love cheer too."

The two performed a mini wave and then hurried inside together. Addison was sure she had just made a new friend.

As for Zed, he was pretty sure he'd like his new school. Once the Zombie Patrol guard let them in!

CHAPTER 4

Once the last human kid was inside, the zombie kids were finally allowed to go into the school.

"Come on, Eliza," Zed said cheerfully as they walked up the front steps. "We're in a real school! No more classes in a dingy basement."

But once the zom-kids were inside the building, they were led all the way downstairs—to a basement classroom for zombies only!

"You were saying?" Eliza muttered.

After everyone was seated at dusty, rusty desks, a woman wearing a three-piece power suit stepped to the head of the class. Without a hint of a smile, she began to speak. "I'm Principal Lee. We are thrilled to be forced to have you here. Do not leave the basement. Have a great year."

A great year for Zed meant playing football for the Mighty Shrimp. So his hand shot up in the air.

"Principal Lee," Zed said with a grin. "I was just wondering . . ."

The principal hated having to spend a moment longer among the zombies. She raised a brow at Zed as if to say, "Yes, get on with it."

"How do I try out for the football team?" Zed continued.

"And the computer coding club?" Eliza blurted out.

"Gruzik?" Bonzo grunted.

Zed caught the principal staring at Bonzo, so he quickly translated. "And music classes," he said. "Bonzo's an artist. He's classically trained."

To demonstrate, the artsy zombie blew his handmade trumpet and gave a yodel. Principal Lee was not impressed but felt inclined to answer her students' questions, even though they were zombies.

"Would any of that involve you leaving the basement?" she asked coolly.

Zed shrugged and said, "Yeah . . . I guess."

"Well, then no tryouts for you!" Principal Lee

snapped. "I'm sorry. I don't mean it. Have a great day. That's just an expression."

The zom-kids watched openmouthed as their principal left the room. And they called zombies rotten. Geez!

Eliza shot Zed an "I told you so" look. Sure, zombies had finally been accepted into a human school. But were the humans accepting of zombies? No way!

Mr. Zeck, a zombie teacher, took the principal's place at the head of the class.

"Okay," Mr. Zeck mumbled. "Let's do grammar or something."

"This is supposed to be chemistry," Eliza said.

Mr. Zeck rolled his eyes up to the leaky ceiling. "Forty-five minutes ago, I was the janitor, kid," he sighed. "So bear with me."

The zom-kids groaned under their breath. So far, Seabrook High was enough to make them go back to eating brains. But there was only one thing on Zed's brain—the Mighty Shrimp football tryouts!

Zed had to try out for the team no matter what. And the first step was to get out of that zombie basement!

Mr. Zeck hardly noticed or cared as Zed slipped

out of the classroom. He climbed the staircase to the main floor and walked down a long hallway. A poster for the cheer tryouts hung on the wall. Next to it was another poster for the football tryouts!

With classes in session, the halls were empty and quiet. Zed knew that sneaking out to the football tryouts was risky, but as he told himself, "I've got smarts and stealth on my side!"

Carefully and quietly, Zed made his way down the hall. So far, so good—until he knocked into a rack of brochures, stubbing his big toe!

"Ahhhh!" he yelled as he tripped.

Zed's toe throbbed and his heart raced. Just when he thought things couldn't get worse, a human student spotted him. Seeing a limping zombie dragging his foot caused her to shout, "Rogue zombie!"

Zed tried explaining that he wasn't a vicious zombie invader, but it was no use. The girl hit the Zombie Alert button, sending an earsplitting siren through the entire school!

As the Z-Alarm blasted, students screamed and raced through the halls. Zed's heart sank when he realized they were running away from him!

"Oh, come on, guys!" Zed called. "Really?"

CHAPTER 5

The Z-Alarm kept blaring, and the kids kept running. To escape the chaos, Zed ran too, but just as he reached the end of the hall, a group of football players rounded the corner.

A Mighty Shrimp lineman took one look at Zed and shouted, "There! Zombie!"

Zed groaned under his breath. Great.

Meanwhile, deep down in the basement, a classroom of zombies wondered what the alarm meant. Could there be a fire? Fire was not a zombie's friend!

"Stay calm. Everything is okay," Mr. Zeck said

blankly. "There is no fire." But he didn't look too sure.

"Fiiiiiire?" Bonzo gasped.

"Fire?" Mr. Zeck cried, looking around. "Where?"

Eliza knew what the alarm was all about. She turned to Bonzo and said, "It's the Z-Alarm, no fire. We zombies have come too far to still be afraid of . . ." With a gulp, Eliza finished her sentence: "Fire."

"Fiiiiiire!" Bonzo shouted.

Before Eliza could stop him, Bonzo jumped up. He bolted toward the door, pulling the doorknob hard. The door whammed into his face, knocking him to the floor with a THUD! Eliza sighed.

The siren kept blaring as a commanding voice came over the PA system: "Rouge zombies will be neutralized!"

The zombie students froze in their seats. Neutralized? That had to hurt.

Suddenly, all eyes turned to the door as four guards burst into the classroom.

"Against the wall!" the Zombie Patrol guard shouted.

This can't be happening! Eliza thought as she and her classmates lined up. She turned to the Zombie Patrol guard and said, "These drills are offensive and driven by zombiephobia!"

"No talking!" the Zombie Patrol guard snapped.

Eliza bit her tongue. Bonzo was still down for the count. But where was Zed? And was he okay?

While zom-kids were detained, human kids scrambled for safety. Most of the panicky students charged up the stairs. Addison and Bree had other plans as they raced downstairs toward the cafeteria.

"I know this is scary, Bree," Addison said, "but there's a safe room in the cafeteria."

Zed was already rushing into the cafeteria, looking for a place to hide from the ferocious football players.

As the girls entered the cafeteria, Bree spotted Zed behind Addison's back. With a piercing scream, she ran back up the stairs.

"Bree, come back!" Addison called.

At the same time, Zed spotted a sign on a nearby door. It read ZOMBIE SAFE ROOM. Could it be a room where zombies were safe? Perfect!

Zed rushed through the door. Addison rushed in too, through another entrance. After shutting the door behind her, an automated voice droned, "Safe room secure!"

The room was dark, lit only by a flashing red light.

As Addison looked around, she could see shelves filled with zombie survival gear. No surprise there. It was a room for a possible zombie outbreak.

Just when Addison thought she was alone, she heard a bump. It seemed to be coming from the other side of the room.

"Hello?" she called out.

"Hello?" Zed's voice called back.

Addison didn't see Zed hiding behind a cluttered shelf. Zed peered through the zombie-fighting paraphernalia to see a girl. It was the same girl he had seen before school.

"Why, hello!" Zed said.

Who said that? Addison spun around to see the shadowy silhouette of a boy behind the shelf. "Don't get any ideas, buster!" she shouted. "The only thing more deadly than my high kick is my low kick!"

"Sorry!" Zed blurted. "This is not how I was expecting my first day in a new school to go."

"You weren't expecting to be trapped in a Zombie Safe Room?" Addison asked.

"That I expected," Zed joked. "It happens to me all the time. It's sort of . . . my thing."

Addison smiled as she stood on the opposite

side of the shelf. She didn't know that the boy was a zombie. She just knew that he sounded nice and funny.

"So I'm not going to get kicked?" Zed asked.

"You're safe for now," Addison chuckled.

"Good, because today's a big day," Zed said. "I'm trying out for football."

"We're both having big days," Addison said excitedly. "I'm trying out for the cheer squad!"

"Wow," Zed said. "That's a tough gig."

"Yeah, but I love it," Addison explained. "My parents have had me in cheer camp since forever."

"My dad doesn't think I'll even make the football team," Zed said.

"Sure you will!" Addison told him. "You just need someone to cheer for you. Soon—fingers crossed—that'll be my job!"

The zom-boy and human girl were still silhouetted as they met at the end of the shelf. In the dimness of the flashing light, they made their introductions:

"I'm Zed. What's your name?"

"Addison. Nice to meet you."

At that moment, the Z-Alarm stopped. The flashing red light became a stark white one. Addison gasped when she saw who she had been talking to all this time. . . .

"Ahhhhh!" Addison screamed. "Zombie!"

Her arm swung back instinctively and then forward as she clocked a surprised Zed straight in the jaw!

"Ow!" Zed exclaimed. So much for safe rooms!

Addison stared as Zed rubbed his jaw. What had she done?

CHAPTER 6

Addison felt awful. She wasn't a violent person. The only thing she ever hit was her mark in cheerleading!

"Omigosh, Zed," Addison blurted. "I am so sorry."

Zed's head was still spinning as he tried to speak.

"My parents taught me that zombies are disgusting, dead-eyed freaks," Addison went on. "But you're not hideous at all."

"I'll take that," Zed managed to say.

Addison felt the need to explain further. "You see, my family's hated zombies ever since one of them bit my grandpa's ear off."

Biting ears off? Zed frowned. That was so old-school!

"Fair," Zed said as he lifted his wrist. "But thanks to the Z-Band, now we'll just talk your ear off."

Addison smiled at Zed's joke. Her smile turned into a frown as the door electronically unbolted and in walked the last person she wanted to see right now. Her cousin Bucky!

"There you are, Addison," Bucky said.

The Aceys followed Bucky into the safe room. Taking one look at Zed, they totally lost it.

"Ewwwww!" Stacey cried.

"Naaaasty!" Tracey chimed in.

"Zombie germs!" Lacey exclaimed.

Zed had a feeling this wasn't good—especially when Bucky grabbed him by the collar.

"If you ever go near my cousin again, it won't be pretty," Bucky warned Zed. "Which, as you can see, is off-brand for me."

Bucky let go of Zed and reached for a spritz of hand sanitizer. Once he was thoroughly disinfected, he threw Zed one last threatening glare. "Now, let's go to the cheer tryouts," he told the Aceys and Addison.

Addison gave Zed a little wave as the Aceys

dragged her toward the door. Once she was out of the room, Zed rubbed his still-aching jaw.

Despite the shocker of a hit, he and Addison seemed to really hit it off. And that was pretty awesome!

"Progress," Zed told himself. "We're making progress."

Zed left the Zombie Safe Room and headed to the football field. He tried to blend in with the other wannabe players, which for a green-haired zombie dude wasn't easy.

A tired-looking guy wearing sweats blew a whistle. Zed guessed he was the Mighty Shrimp coach.

"Welcome to the football tryouts," Coach announced in a weary voice. "As you know, this town is a cheerleading town 'cause this town likes to win. And our football team is awful. We're not going to win this year. And I'll probably lose my job."

With a sigh, Coach then said, "Good news for you, though. You've all made the team. Whoopee."

Zed pumped his fist. The tone was off, but the message was crystal clear. "Yes!" Zed cheered under his breath. "Made it!"

He was about to high-five the guy next to him

when Coach added, "Except for the zombie."

Zed froze. Whaaaaaat??

"Principal Lee said you guys aren't even supposed to leave the basement. She didn't tell you?"

"I don't think so. I would've remembered that," Zed lied. "Come on, please just let me be on the team?"

But Coach shook his head. "Can't have a zombie on my field," he insisted. "We'd be a laughingstock."

Zed's heart sank and his shoulders drooped. What good was going to a human school when you couldn't even play football!

It was back to the basement for Zed and his zombuds. As they walked through the hall toward their classroom, Zed described what had happened at the football tryouts.

"Football's stupid anyway," Eliza grumbled.

"Thanks for the pep talk," Zed said. "But you know, I think that cheerleader likes me."

Eliza stared, horrified at Zed. "The one that punched you?" she cried, "In the face?"

"Yeah," Zed said with a smile. "There's something there."

Eliza rolled her eyes. What was *not* there was common sense! "You're delusional, Zed," she said.

"Humans are bad, but cheerleaders are monsters!"

Zed agreed that things for zombies still had to change. But he knew that not all humans were bad.

He also knew one cheerleader who was definitely not a monster—Addison!

CHAPTER 7

"**O**kay, let's go!" Bucky shouted. "Welcome to cheerleading tryouts!"

Addison stood in the gym next to Bree. This was the moment they had been waiting for. If all went well, they would be on the Mighty Shrimp cheer squad!

Bucky looked around the gym. "Nice to see so many wannabes," he said. "We'd wannabe us too if we weren't already on the squad."

The Aceys giggled at Bucky's joke, then stopped on cue.

"I'm too nervous," Bree whispered.

Addison smiled at her new friend. "Bree," she said gently, "you're going to rock this."

Bree remained glum. Especially when Bucky introduced his assistant captains . . .

"Stacey! Lacey! Tracey!" Bucky shouted. "The Aceys!"

The wannabes watched openmouthed as each Acey flipped or somersaulted to their name.

"Let's keep this simple," Bucky announced. "You just have to do one little itsy-bitsy move and you're on our squad. Easy-peasy."

Relieved sighs filled the gym. Addison and Bree traded thankful smiles. These tryouts would be just like Bucky said—easy-peasy. But when Bucky explained what he wanted them to do, they became queasy!

"A back-handspring-funky-chicken-roundoff-mashed-potato-split with a robot-powering-down finish!" he declared.

A bunch of long-faced wannabes started heading toward the door. Addison frowned. How could they give up so soon?

"Sadly, almost none of you will make the team," Bucky threw in. "But don't feel bad. There are other ways to bring cheer to the world." He shrugged and continued, "I can't think of any right now, but science is making leaps and bounds."

Addison was finally going to show what years and years of summer cheer camp taught her. She turned toward her cousin and spoke up. "Captain Bucky? Was that funky chicken Cajun or Shake 'n Bake?"

Bucky gave it a thought. "Never seen Cajun," he admitted. "Spice it up."

Addison grabbed Bree's hand. "We got this," she whispered.

Addison and Bree followed every move as Bucky led the wannabes in a routine, backed up by Stacey, Lacey, and Tracey.

They were no longer intimidated by the Aceys or Bucky. All they were was fired up, even as Bucky began the elimination process. . . .

"No, no, no," Bucky sang out, pointing to each disappointing reject. He kept eliminating until there was only a handful of people left—including Addison and Bree.

Addison turned to Bree and smiled. It was happening—it was really happening! She had been waiting for this moment since she was a little girl.

Bree had plenty to smile about too. Many times she had been told to forget about making the cheer squad. She was glad she listened to her heart, and to Addison!

But suddenly, there was a new challenge. Bucky lowered a giant curtain with the words FEARLESS NOT CHEERLESS to reveal a bunch of students crowded on the bleachers. "You guys have got moves," he said. "But can you win over a crowd? Get them to worship you like they worship me!"

Addison and Bree totally killed it as the spectators applauded and cheered. "We're fired up! You're fired up! We're fired up!"

Bucky walked over to his cousin. "Welcome to the Mighty Shrimp, Addison. Wear our colors with pride."

"Yes!" Addison agreed. "Yes, yes."

As she hugged Bucky, Addison noticed Bree's sad smile. "Hey, Cuz, Bree over there has great moves and serious pep."

"Seabrook is all about precision," Bucky said firmly. "And perfection." He lowered his voice. "She can't hide her flaws under a wig like some people."

Ouch. Addison gulped, remembering her secret silvery hair. "Pretty please?" she asked her cousin.

Bucky's nostrils flared as he seemed to think about it. He then forced his famous dazzling-white smile. Turning from Addison to Bree, he said, "You made the squad . . . as a stand-in."

In a flash, the Aceys were in Bree's face.

"Stay out of my light," Lacey growled.

"Cheer toward the edges," Stacey warned.

"In case we need to crop you from the team photos," Tracey snapped.

"What? I'm on the team?" Bree gasped with surprise. "Yes! Yes! Woo!"

Bree ran over to Addison for a celebratory Shrimp shimmy dance. Bucky cocked his head in amusement as he watched his new recruits.

"Yes, people love cheer." Bucky grinned. "It's what makes me so important—and I'd hate to see that change." His smile seemed to fade immediately. "But change is in the air since zombies entered our school. Cheer is being threatened," Bucky explained to the new team members. "Are you ready to protect it?"

He raised a fist in the air and shouted, "Let cheer initiation begin!"

Addison and Bree exchanged worried looks. What did zombies have to do with the cheer squad initiation?

CHAPTER 8

Later that night, Addison gazed out the window of the cheer van as they pulled in to Zombietown.

Bucky and the Aceys remained in the van. Addison and Bree stepped out to look around.

"Zombietown," Addison said softly. "Wow."

Zombietown was an old, run-down neighborhood. But as Addison and Bree looked closer, they could see it was far from bleak—and almost magical!

There were no modern streetlights. Instead, old-timey bulbs inside rusted birdcages dangled from trees. Several structures in the neighborhood seemed to be made from repurposed materials and built with love.

Addison looked across the street. A little girl was sitting among a garden of illuminated flowers. She did not yet know that the girl was Zoey—just that the scene was beautiful!

Addison turned at the sound of Bucky's voice. Her cousin was still inside the van as he spoke through the window.

"Every year for cheer initiation, we like to remind zombies that we don't accept freaks in this town," Bucky told Bree and Addison. He leaned out the window to hand them a carton of eggs. "Egg that zombie house and you're both officially one of us."

What? Addison practically dropped the carton when she heard what Bucky wanted them to do. No way would she maliciously egg a zombie house. And she knew Bree wouldn't either.

"No, we can't do that," Addison said.

She was about to explain why when a zombie woman lumbered over. She smiled with rotting teeth at the kids inside the van. "You look lost," she said. "Can I help you?"

"Ahhhhh!" Bucky and the Aceys screamed at the sight of the zombie.

They stepped on the gas and totally floored it. The van zoomed off, leaving Addison and Bree alone in Zombietown!

Feeling vulnerable, the girls hid behind a pile of debris. They peeked out to see front doors swinging open and zombies emerging from their houses.

Most of them addressed the zombie who was trying to help, all talking at once: "Any trouble?" "Cheerleaders causing problems again?" "We got your back."

Addison's eyes widened at the sight of Zed rushing out of his house. As he made his way to the street, another zombie stepped outside onto the porch. Addison guessed it was Zed's dad.

"Everything okay out there?" Zevon called out.

Addison gazed down at the egg carton in her hand. Things were definitely not okay.

"This is not good," Bree whispered.

Zed turned to see Addison and Bree peeking out from behind the junk pile. A second later, Zevon called out from the porch, "Hey, Zed? Anyone there?"

Addison held her breath as she and Zed made eye contact. After a few awkward seconds, Zed turned toward his dad. "No," he called back. "Nobody."

"Come back inside, then," Zevon said.

Zed shot Addison a disappointed look. He walked over to Zoey, took her hand, and led her into the house. After Zevon gave the neighborhood one last glance, he entered the house too.

Addison felt sad as she and Bree stepped out of the shadows. "Are zombies always being harassed?" she asked. "I had no idea life was this bad for them."

She frowned at the carton of eggs still in her hands and knew just where to toss them—in a garbage can!

CHAPTER 9

The next day, as Addison walked to school, she saw zombies waiting behind the fence, just as they did every morning. But today she saw her zombie classmates with fresh eyes.

The night before, Addison had realized that zombies cared for the same things humans did—their families, friends, and communities. So why were they treated like second-class citizens? It just wasn't fair!

Addison ran to catch up with Bucky as he breezed past the fence.

"Zombies are students at Seabrook High School,

Bucky," Addison told him. "Picking on them isn't right."

"Zombies distract people from what's really important," Bucky argued. "Cheer. Us. Me."

"But we can't go around tormenting them!" Addison declared.

Bucky sighed. "It's best that you don't question things, okay?" He flashed an encouraging grin. "Pep rally today, Cuz. We're gonna rock it!"

Addison watched her cousin head toward the school with pep in his step. For the first time, she felt no spirit at all—just frustration as she grabbed the fence and gave it a shake!

Zed was feeling just as frustrated as he walked through the basement with his friends. "In addition to getting rejected from football, I met a cheerleader," he said as they entered their classroom. "I thought she was cool, and different, but I was wrong. Cheerleaders are all terrible."

Zed was about to sit down when he heard Mr. Zeck say, "Sorry, no human students in the basement."

Human students? Where?

All the zom-kids turned to see a human girl with long blond hair standing at the door. It was Addison!

"Someone just yakked in the cafeteria," Addison told Mr. Zeck.

Still the janitor, Mr. Zeck grabbed his mop and bucket and trudged toward the door. "Everyone keep learning things," he mumbled before leaving the classroom.

Addison didn't follow Mr. Zeck. Instead, she walked into the room and looked around. Her eyes were wide as they scanned the peeling paint, leaky ceiling, and dust-covered furniture.

"This is . . . awful!" Addison gasped.

"Would have cleaned," Eliza joked, "but our teacher's territorial about his mop."

"Addison," Zed said. "What are you doing here?"

"Apologizing," Addison explained. "My cousin is a jerk about zombies. And last night was cheer initiation." Her shoulders drooped. "Not that that's a good excuse. I'm so sorry."

Zed accepted Addison's apology. But it wasn't Addison he was worried about. "What if Bucky sees us talking?" he asked.

"We'll make sure he doesn't," Addison promised. "See you at the pep rally this afternoon?"

"Zombies don't do pep rallies," Eliza said.

Zed gave Eliza a look and turned back to Addison. "We'll think about it," he told her.

Addison gave a little wave and a smile as she turned toward the door.

"Somebody crack a window," Eliza muttered. "It stinks of human."

But Zed didn't hear Eliza. He was too busy watching Addison glide out of the classroom. True, zombies didn't go to pep rallies. But there was a first time for everything!

Later, in the cheer lounge, everyone was getting ready for the pep rally.

As cheerleaders curled, flat-ironed, spritzed, and glossed their hair, Addison tried not to think about her cute zombie friend. But it was hopeless—she totally had Zed in her head!

"Of course Zed's not coming," Addison reasoned to herself. "Zombies at a cheer rally would be serious drama!"

With that, Bree peeked out the door at the gym. The bleachers were filled to the max with friends, family . . . and a few unexpected guests!

"There are zombies at the pep rally!" Bree gasped.

Zombies? Addison turned away from the mirror to stare at Bree. Zombies—as in Zed?

"They wouldn't dare!" Bucky sneered.

Bucky, Addison, and the Aceys raced to the door to peek out too. Sure enough, Zed, Eliza, and Bonzo were heading toward the bleachers. When Addison saw Zed, her heart turned a triple flip.

But Bucky's eyes burned at the zombies in the stands. He would show those brain-munching, puppy-chasing, dead-eyed monsters—and make sure they never dragged their decaying flesh into the Seabrook gym again!

"Stacey, Lacey, Tracey," Bucky said through gritted teeth. "Bust out the spirit sticks!"

CHAPTER 10

The cheerleaders weren't the only ones surprised to see zombies in the stands. A hush fell over the gym as the crowd spotted Zed, Eliza, and Bonzo. Many stretched their necks to get a look at the "zombie freaks."

An angry Eliza turned to Zed. "I can't believe you dragged us here to see Cheery McCheerstein," she hissed. "Makes me sick. Do I look green? I mean, greener than usual?"

Zed didn't regret coming to the pep rally. He wanted to show support for the Mighty Shrimp—even if they didn't support him. He was about to answer

Eliza when music blasted and a colossal banner fluttered down from the ceiling. It was a banner of Bucky, striking his signature cheer pose.

The fanfare built up until Bucky himself burst through the banner. The crowd went wild as their cheer idol addressed them through a megaphone: "Welcome to the Seabrook High pep rally! This is going to be an amazing year!"

Bucky raised his voice for effect. "We're going to win the state cheer championship again! And we can't do it without me! Let's hear it for me!"

"Bu-cky! Bu-cky! Bu-cky!" his fans shouted.

"At this time," Bucky went on, "I'd like to present to you this year's cheer squad."

The Aceys, Addison, and the rest of the team flipped into the gym to wild applause. They did a routine of acrobatic tricks, fierce flips, sensational splits, and sky-high toe touches.

Bree stood to the side, shaking her pom-poms to the pulsating electronic beat. With such a flawless routine, it was easy for the crowd to see who put the pep in the pep rally—the Mighty Shrimp cheer squad!

"*Ragrazock!*" Bonzo cheered.

Eliza elbowed Bonzo in the ribs. Since when was he a cheerleading fanboy?

"Ease up, Eliza," Zed said with a smile. "Cheerleading's contagious."

"So is pink eye," she grumbled.

The excitement in the gym grew and grew. The Aceys and Addison circled Bucky, shaking silver pom-poms in perfect rhythm. With the drama at its peak, Bucky whipped out a spirit stick. A bright flaming spark shot from it, high into the air.

"Let's turn up the heat!" Bucky cried.

The zombie kids did not see this coming. The sight of the fire caused them to tremble in their seats.

"Deep breath, guys," Zed murmured, trying to hold it together. "That fire is not going to hurt us."

Zed, Eliza, and Bonzo tried hard not to panic as Bucky twirled the flaming stick like a baton.

Bucky had hate in his eyes as he shouted, "Let everybody see them for what they really are—monsters!"

The faster Bucky twirled, the bigger the flame grew.

Bonzo shuddered. "F-f-f-iiiiiire!" he cried.

"We're going to be okay, buddy," Zed said.

But Zed's words had no effect on his freaked-out friend. Bonzo leaped up from his seat and charged down the stands. In a fit of fear, Bonzo knocked Zed aside. As Zed stumbled, his Z-Band banged on the ground and began flashing UNSTABLE.

In the middle of the chaos, three male cheerleaders launched Addison into the air. They positioned themselves for the catch, but then ran off screaming as Bonzo raced right toward them!

"Bonzo! No!" Zed shouted.

With his Z-Band out of whack, Zed's eyes blazed and his veins bulged as tremendous energy coursed up his arms. Zed was zombie-ing out!

The crowd gasped as Addison plunged toward the ground with no one to catch her. That was when Zed sprang into action. With uncanny strength and speed, he leaped over humans, zigzagged around cheerleaders, and barreled through the football team.

Everyone, including the football coach, watched as the zombie plunged underneath Addison just in time to make the perfect catch. The impact set Zed's Z-Band back to normal as he gently placed Addison on the ground.

As Zed and Addison stared into each other's eyes, the coach's voice boomed out. "You. Me. We gotta talk. The principal's office—now, Zed!"

"He knocked aside our offensive lineman, Principal Lee," Coach said. "Like they were scrawny freshmen!"

Zed sat in the principal's office, knowing he was in deep trouble. "Principal Lee," he pleaded, "let me explain—"

"Coach wants you on his team," Principal Lee cut in.

Zed stared at the principal, then at the coach. "Really?"

Coach nodded. "With a monster . . . er . . . a monster player like you, we can turn the football team around."

Zed was too stunned to speak. Was this really happening?

"I need you on my team, Zed," Coach admitted. "Say you'll do it."

Zed grinned at the magic words. It was happening! He was a zombie playing ball for the Mighty Shrimp! But Zed realized this could also be an amazing opportunity for all zom-kind. Instead of answering yes right away, he had a request. "I can only agree if there are some changes," Zed said. "Full integration for all zombies."

"There's just one little problem," Principal Lee said. "You haven't won a game yet."

"That's a mere technicality," Zed said with all the cockiness of Seabrook's newest football star.

Coach turned to Principal Lee. "Can you throw my star player a bone?" he asked. "Not literally, of course."

Principal Lee gave it some thought, then looked straight at Zed. "In a show of good faith," she said, "I will allow zombies to eat in the cafeteria."

Zed smiled. Nice!

"And then if you start racking up some wins, we'll talk about your other demands."

"You've got yourself a deal!" Zed declared.

"Deal," Coach agreed. "See you at practice, Zed."

Not everyone was happy with the deal. Outside the principal's office stood Bucky, listening and watching the whole thing from behind the glass.

"Nooooo!" Bucky cried, sliding down the wall.

But as Zed left the principal's office, he was ready to perform a victory dance. He might not have scored for the Mighty Shrimps yet, but he just scored for the zombies—big-time!

CHAPTER 11

The next morning, Zed went to school with a spring in his step and joy in his heart. He wasn't just a zombie—he was the ultimate dealmaker! But would his demands for all zombie students really be met?

Later that day, an announcement over the PA system confirmed that change had finally come.

"As you may have heard," Principal Lee's voice stated, "zombie students are now allowed to eat in the cafeteria."

The humans in the cafeteria erupted in protest. "Zombies, ewwww!" "Gross!" "Oh no! Does my face look delicious?" "I don't want to eat with a freak!"

"Just deal with it," Principal Lee said.

All eyes turned to the door as it burst open. Outside the door was a crowd of zombie students looking in.

"The human cafeteria," Eliza whispered. "Zed, you really delivered."

Led by Zed, the zombies strutted into the cafeteria, heading straight for their own tables.

"Great," Eliza said. "Our own lunch table in the dankest corner under cheap fluorescent lights—next to the trash!" These were considered five-star eating accommodations for a zombie!

"It's perfect," Zed agreed. "We're livin' large and in charge!"

At the other side of the cafeteria, Addison and Bree were eating lunch. But one girl was doing more talking than eating. . . .

"I love the thought of flying through the air," Bree babbled. "Oxygen is so underrated. So is dirt. I hate doing dishes but love soap." She turned to Addison and said, "Weird, right?"

Addison wasn't looking at Bree or her lunch. She was gazing across the cafeteria at the adorable zombie guy who had saved her at the pep rally the day before.

"Weird that my heart's racing and my palms are sweaty?" Addison asked dreamily.

"Oh no!" Bree said, touching Addison's forehead. "You have the flu."

Addison shook her head. "It's not the flu, Bree," she said. "It's Zed."

Bree tapped her chin thoughtfully as she tried to sort it out. Addison's heart was racing, her palms were sweating . . .

Bree's eyes lit up as it suddenly clicked. Addison was crushing on Zed!

"Wait, you like him?" Bree asked. "You like-like a zombie? Wow."

"That's bad, right?" Addison asked. "Really bad. My parents would so freak out. Are we still friends?"

"Hello!" Bree declared with a smile. "I have your back, no matter what. I just don't want anyone to break your heart . . . or devour it." She then held up her hand and said, "I swear on all I hold dear—mostly glitter lip balm—that I will tell nobody!"

Addison smiled at her new friend's loyalty. It felt good to share her feelings about Zed. But what if her feelings were just a waste of time?

"Nothing is going to happen," Addison sighed. "He probably doesn't even remember my name—"

"Addison!" a voice cut in.

Addison whipped her head around to see Zed waving to her from across the cafeteria. Not only did he remember her name—he seemed to want to invite her over!

Her heart racing faster and her palms even sweatier, Addison rose from her chair. "I can't be rude," she told Bree.

A hush fell over the cafeteria as Addison crossed over to the zombie side. Once there, she addressed the zombie students with a smile and a special greeting. "As they say in old zombie tongue, *Nagrazutty rargrazain stargrazick*." Upon seeing their blank stares she added, "I looked it up on the internet."

"You just thanked me for rubbing peanut butter on your umbrella," Zed chuckled.

"Oh!" Addison said, feeling her cheeks burn. "I meant welcome to the cafeteria!"

Bonzo held up the apple he had carved into an elaborate rose shape. Addison smiled as Bonzo handed it to her.

"Uh, why is Perky Von Cheerstick here?" Eliza demanded. "The point of having our own table is to avoid people like her!"

Addison flinched. Maybe it wasn't a great idea to visit the zombie table. "Oh, I just wanted to say thanks to Zed," she said quickly, "for rescuing me—"

Addison stopped mid-sentence as the Aceys grabbed her arms. The apple rose flew out of her hands as Stacey, Lacey, and Tracey began dragging Addison away from the zombie table.

Back at the human side of the cafeteria, the Aceys surrounded Addison.

"You're talking to a zombie?" Tracey demanded.

"I'm fighting intolerance!" Addison admitted.

"I fought mine by eliminating dairy," Lacey sniffed.

"Zombie intolerance," Addison corrected her. Why was her friendship with Zed any of the Aceys' business? It had nothing to do with cheer . . . or did it?

"Your cousin's not going to be happy you're palling around with zombies," Lacey declared.

"Cheerleaders don't support freaks!" Stacey said.

Tracey cocked his head as he eyed Addison.

"Right. . . . Bucky said there was something different about you," he said slowly. "I can see that now."

See what? Addison felt a chill run up her back. Was a wisp of her secret silvery hair hanging out? Wasn't her wig on straight?

"I'm not different," Addison insisted.

The Aceys were determined to see for themselves. They began circling Addison, looking her up and down.

"Your smile?" Lacey wondered. "Is that an overbite?"

"Is one leg longer than the other?" Stacey asked slowly.

"Oh no!" Tracey said, staring into Addison's eyes. "Do you wear corrective lenses?"

Addison bit her lip. There was nothing wrong with overbites, uneven legs, or corrective lenses—unless you lived in Seabrook!

"No, no, no, I'm not different," Addison insisted. "I'm the same-est person you've ever met."

That didn't seem to matter to the Aceys. Addison had paid a visit to the zombie table—and that was strictly taboo!

"Hanging with zombies is hazardous," Lacey said.

"You could end up at the reject table like *that*!" She snapped her fingers in Addison's face.

Addison had gotten the message. Loud and clear. She had also heard enough. Turning away from the Aceys, she headed straight toward the door.

Zed had seen everything from the zombie table. He grabbed Bonzo's apple rose and headed for the door too—to catch up with Addison!

CHAPTER 12

Addison walked away from the cafeteria and through the hall, her heart racing and her palms sweaty once again. But this time it wasn't because of her feelings for Zed. It was from her nightmarish encounter with the Aceys.

How dare they tell her who she couldn't like or be friends with! Who did Bucky think he was, other than Seabrook High's superstar head cheerleader, adored by all?

Addison had a sick feeling that if she wanted to

stay on the cheer squad, she would have to stay away from zombies, mainly Zed. But how could she do that if Zed was still inside her head . . . and now just a few feet away from her in the hall?

"Ah, the perfect picnic spot," Zed's voice said as he walked toward Addison.

Addison smiled. He stopped to hand her Bonzo's apple rose. She accepted it appreciatively.

"The hall does have a certain . . . what's the word?" she asked.

"Stench?" Zed offered.

Addison laughed and joined Zed. For both, it felt good to be away from all the cafeteria drama.

"Sorry I couldn't sit with you in the cafeteria," Addison told Zed as they walked through the empty hallway. "I wanted to . . . just everyone was—"

"I get it," Zed cut in. "Someday, maybe."

Addison remembered what she had wanted to tell Zed in the cafeteria, before she was pulled away by the cheerless cheerleaders. "Thanks for saving me at the pep rally."

"It worked out for everyone," Zed told her. "I'm going to be on the football team, and if I do well, maybe zombies will be more accepted and we could hang out together in public."

"That would be really something," Addison sighed. "This school. This town. It's hard not fitting in."

Addison's words surprised Zed. She wasn't a zombie. She was a human girl on the cheer squad. If that wasn't fitting in, he'd eat his fingers!

"How would you know?" Zed asked gently. "You're perfect."

Addison gave her long blond hair a tug. "It's a wig," she said. "My real hair is freakish, and I can't change it."

Freakish? Now Zed was curious.

"Can I see it?" he asked.

"Never," Addison said. "My parents have always made me cover my hair. And they're right." She threw back her shoulders and added, "Because now I'm on the cheer squad. And I fit in!"

For the first time, Zed felt bad for Addison. Didn't she know she was perfect, whatever that "freakish" stuff under her wig was?

"You shouldn't have to hide who you really are," Zed said, "especially when you're awesome."

"I wish I had your confidence," Addison said. It felt good to talk honestly with a friend, and Zed was quickly becoming one of her best.

The sudden sound of voices told Addison and Zed they were not alone. Knowing they couldn't be seen together, Zed swung open the nearest door.

Once inside the small room, Addison looked around and smiled. They were back in the Zombie Safe Room. "This is where we met," she told Zed.

"Where we had our first punch," Zed teased, rubbing his jaw.

Addison giggled. Oh, yeah. That.

With no flashing red lights, the room was totally dark. Zed found the only lamp in the room and turned it on. It was just an old light bulb stuck on a pole, but it cast the warmest glow.

It was then Zed became more optimistic than ever. If only Addison would get to know him, things could work out. Someday there could be movie dates, walks in the park, hanging wherever they wanted to.

Grabbing the light pole, Zed did a little dance. Addison joined in, in perfect sync. They made great dance partners. Maybe someday they would take their dance out in the open and show the world how similar zombies and humans really were.

Addison no longer cared what the Aceys or her

It's a beautiful day in Zombietown.
Zed is excited to go to his new school—with humans!

Eliza, Zed, and Bonzo find out that zombies aren't allowed to leave the basement.

Addison and Bree are ready for cheerleading tryouts.

Bucky is the cheer captain.

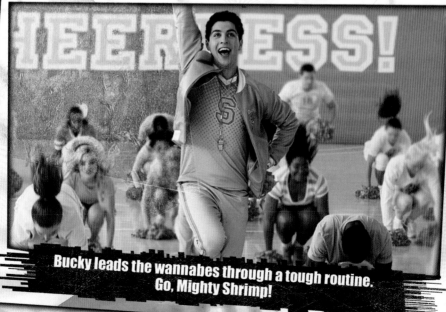

Bucky leads the wannabes through a tough routine.
Go, Mighty Shrimp!

For cheer initiation, Bucky wants Addison and Bree to throw eggs at zombie houses.

Zed's dream comes true—he's on the football team!

Bree and Addison cheer for Zed. Bucky does not approve.

Zed tells Addison that his Z-band helps him win games.

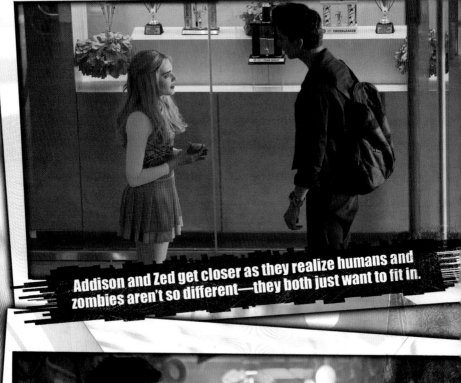

Addison and Zed get closer as they realize humans and zombies aren't so different—they both just want to fit in.

Zed invites Addison to a zombie mash.

Bonzo gets the music going!

Zed and his friends dance and celebrate until the zombie curfew.

At the Cheer Championship, Zoey tells Bucky not to give up.

Humans and zombies make a great team!

cousin Bucky thought. Let them talk if they wanted to. She and Zed were going to do what they wanted, where they wanted.

She took Zed's hand and led him out of the room just as the bell rang. Students spilled into the hall, rushing to their next classes.

"Time for class," Zed whispered as they moved apart.

"Good luck at the football game," Addison whispered back.

Zed looked over his shoulder as he hurried to class. "It's going to be awesome!"

CHAPTER 13

"Oof!" Zed grunted.

Things didn't seem so awesome when a beefy linebacker shook Zed upside down like a clogged ketchup bottle, then slammed him into the turf.

"Oh, that hurts!" the announcer declared. "It's third and long for Seabrook. Really long. The Mighty Shrimp are doing what they do best: losing."

The cheer squad moved perkily together to the grim news. Happiest was Bucky. Turned out the dead-eyed zombie freak was not the football hero Coach and Principal Lee thought he was. What a shame. *Not*.

But not every cheerleader was glad to see Zed get

pummeled. Addison tried hard not to grimace as she whispered under her breath, "Come on, Zed."

Way, way up in the stands sat more of Zed's fans—his zombie family and friends. For Eliza, watching the game was like watching a pyrotechnics display. Not fun. Only Zoey had a blast as she admired the cheerleaders in action.

"At least the cheerleaders are amazing!" Zoey said, clapping her hands.

"We don't clap for cheerleaders," Eliza hissed.

The cheerleaders pepped up the crowd as the Mighty Shrimp lined up with the opposing team. Zed was psyched as he settled behind the quarterback.

"We got this!" Zed declared. "There is no I in 'team,' though there is one in 'zombie.' Teamwork!"

Zed's teammates gazed back blankly as a lineman leaned toward his opponent. "Be my guest," he whispered. "The zombie's all yours."

The ball was hiked. The quarterback handed it off to Zed. Mighty Shrimp linemen stepped aside, giving their opponents a clear path to run at Zed!

Fired up, Zed dodged one attacker and whirled around the next. The crowd had to admit that the zombie was good. Until—WHAM! Zed's face was rammed into the turf. The ball bounced out of his hands, and the opposing team scored a touchdown.

Zed turned his face up from the turf, spitting out a mouthful of dirt. "I detect an earthy undertone with maybe a hint of grass?" From where he lay, Zed saw anti-zombie signs raised by hissing and booing humans. Not a great sign for Zed—or any zombie!

"It's halftime, and the Mighty Shrimp are getting barbecued," the announcer reported. "Skewered. Fried and flayed."

Zed's dad heaved a heavy sigh. "It's going to be a long season," Zevon said.

"Football stinks," Eliza mumbled.

Refusing to give up on her brother, Zoey cheered, "Go, Zed, go!"

But Zed wasn't able to hear his sister's spirit. He was with his team in the locker room, listening to Coach's pepless pep talk.

"Look, I knew we'd be losing," Coach said in his usual deadpan way. "You knew it too, so get out there and lose a little better. Go, team."

The Mighty Shrimp stood up and dragged themselves out of the locker room. But when Zed reached the door, Coach yanked him aside.

"What's happening out there?" Coach demanded.

"Maybe it's team chemistry?" Zed suggested. "Not

sure if the team's blocking for me—"

"We had a deal, Zed!" a voice interrupted.

Zed gulped, recognizing the voice. He turned to see an angry Principal Lee leaning in the doorway.

"You're not keeping your end of it," Principal Lee went on. "Win this game or it's back to the basement."

Zed's arms and legs stiffened as the principal walked away. The future of zombie students at Seabrook was all on him. But no pressure.

"Where's that brute power I saw at the pep rally?" Coach asked.

"Oh," Zed said. "My Z-Band was—"

"Great," Coach cut in. "Just give me more of that."

Zed stared at the coach. Was he serious? "I can't, Coach," he said. "I can't."

Coach refused to listen as he left the locker room. Zed slumped down on a bench, his head in his hands. What had happened at the pep rally was a fluke. The glitch in his Z-Band was totally out of his control.

For once, the optimistic zombie felt totally hopeless—until he was struck by a sudden idea. Maybe what he'd just told Coach wasn't true. Maybe he had more control over his Z-Band than he thought!

CHAPTER 14

"**I**'m not letting you talk me into doing this, Zed," Eliza said, closing her laptop. "It's ludicrously dangerous."

"I just need a little zom-boost," Zed said with an encouraging smile. "Like what happened at the pep rally."

"Because that wasn't a total disaster," Eliza muttered, oozing with sarcasm. She wasn't thrilled with the idea of manipulating Zed's Z-Band and turning him into a dead-boy demolisher.

"You've already jailbroken your Z-Band to play

video games," Zed said. "I thought you could do this too. If I win this game, that's good for us. It's good for zombies, and isn't that what we need?"

Eliza sighed. She opened her laptop and started typing at breakneck speed. She thought out loud as code appeared on her computer screen.

"Whoa, way too unstable," Eliza said. "Eww, too human. Nah, too little. Tad too much. Okay, just a bit more. There!"

Eliza hit a few more keys, then pressed enter. All systems go. She turned to Zed. "Never swipe to the right, okay? That'll corrupt the software," she warned. "Only left. Never right. Got it?"

Zed nodded his head. He got it—and couldn't wait to use it!

"And if you smell smoke," Eliza went on, "stop, drop, and roll."

Zed nodded again. Check.

In just minutes, Zed was back on the field. At the whistle, a herd of opposing defensive linemen charged toward him like bulls seeing red.

Getting no help from his team, Zed swiped left on his Z-Band. In an instant, an excessive surge of power shot up his arms and legs. Feeling every muscle in his body swell, he let out a mighty "ROOOOOAAAAAARRRRR!"

The crowd watched in awe. Zed's eyes were blazing and his muscles were bulging. He plowed through the opposing defense line, flattening them like shrimp omelets as he ran for a touchdown!

Zed whooped as he spiked the ball in the end zone. But as he waited for tremendous cheers, all he heard were crickets and a few surprised claps. Only one fan way up in the nosebleed seats was not afraid to show some love. . . .

"That's my son!" Zevon cheered. "The zombie!"

Even Eliza was psyched. "Is football always humans getting a smackdown?" she asked excitedly. "Count me in and pass the popcorn!"

The zombies had much to celebrate, but the zombie haters were stunned beyond belief. Zed scoring a perfect touchdown was not the tragic ending they had hoped for.

"Dumb luck," Bucky scoffed.

Addison ignored her cousin as she turned a cartwheel, shook her pom-poms, and cheered for Zed. "Oh, feel that breeze—it's not a sneeze! Zombies run and score with ease!"

"Um, what are you doing?" Bucky demanded.

"Cheering," Addison replied. "The football team hasn't won since ever. But we can help change that."

She pointed a pom-pom at the other cheerleaders and said, "I bet the whole squad cheering together could lead the football team to victory. Imagine the joy it would bring."

With a quick tug on Addison's wig, Bucky said, "That kind of accepting, idealistic attitude has no place in cheer!"

He smiled as his usual crowd of fans approached for autographs and selfies.

Addison wanted to keep cheering for Zed, but Bucky had something over her. He knew about her secret silvery hair. Things could get pretty hairy if the rest of Seabrook knew too.

Meanwhile, out on the field, the game was going strong—thanks to a powered-up Zed. The Mighty Shrimp racked up point after point as he scored touchdown after touchdown—until his final touchdown brought the team to victory!

"Seabrook wins!" the announcer exclaimed. "A win!"

The crowd went wild. Zevon and Zoey traded a

hug while Bonzo whooped for joy. Even Eliza rocked a happy dance in the stands.

"The Mighty Shrimp aren't lowest on the food chain anymore," the announcer declared. "Times are changing!"

While Zed reveled in the love and respect, he discreetly adjusted his Z-Band. The extra power in his body fizzled out as he became a normal zombie again.

"Welcome to the team," the Mighty Shrimp lineman told Zed as they headed off the field.

Zed traded a high five with his teammate. Just when he thought things couldn't get better, Addison rushed over.

"Wow," Addison told Zed. "You were amazing."

"Thanks," Zed said. "Awesome cheers."

With that, the football hero and the cheerleader exchanged a hug. Life was definitely good for Zed, the zombie powerhouse. Life was not as good for a fuming Bucky as he watched Addison hug a zombie.

He had always hated those flesh-munching gnat-magnets. But now, with his cousin crushing on one, it was personal!

CHAPTER 15

"Life is good!" Zed declared as he sprinted out of his house the next morning. He stopped to check on the dying flower he had watered. It no longer looked dead and dusty, but fresh, alive, and blooming.

When Zed reached Seabrook High, he saw that his other demands were already being met. A grounds crew was taking down the stupid zombie fence at last.

Zombie students went from zeroes to heroes, thanks to Zed leading his team to victory. Human kids ignored the crusty plates in the nearby dirty-dish bins and flocked to the zombie table in the cafeteria.

"Zed, great game!" "Way to go!" "Awesome win!"

Zed and Bonzo felt like zombie rock stars. But Eliza felt strange as two human kids sat down next to her.

"Being liked is sooooo weird," Eliza told Zed, before cracking a little smile. Weird . . . but kinda cool!

But not all human kids were worshipping the zombie table. Back at the cheer table, Bucky watched with a dropped jaw. Was his mind playing tricks on him, or was he really seeing humans and zombies together?

Another human eager to join the excitement was Addison. She stood up from her chair, ready to visit Zed, but didn't get far. Grabbing her arm, Bucky hissed, "You're either pro-cheerleader or pro-zombie. Decide now."

Addison turned a shocked face to her cousin. "Wait, what?" she cried. "You know how hard I worked for this. You can't—"

"What's it going to be?" Bucky snapped.

Addison's head spun as she weighed the two options. She liked Zed a lot. But she loved cheering more than anything in the world, so . . .

"I . . . I want to be a cheerleader," Addison stammered. "That's all I've ever wanted."

"Good," Bucky stated.

From the other side of the room, Zed caught Addison's eye. He waved to her from the zombie table and called her name.

Addison tried not to cry. She wanted so badly to wave back to Zed. Instead, she turned away.

With a smug smile, Bucky spoke to the Aceys. "This zombie trend will pass. Trust me—the football team won't win another game."

But the Mighty Shrimp scored three wins in a row—thanks to their new football hero, Zombie Zed!

When Bucky saw his own admirers surrounding Zed for autographs and selfies, it was more than he could stand. Zombies were not only taking over the school, they were taking over his loyal fan base.

The last thing Bucky wanted to hear was Principal Lee's latest announcement crackling across the PA system: "Zombies will be joining in all classes and activities," the principal said. "And remember—having a zombie on the football team was my idea."

Zed was still busy signing autographs when Eliza walked by, her computer under her arm.

"I'm off to computer club. Me!" Eliza gasped unbelievingly. "I think I might be . . . happy."

Eliza wasn't the only happy zombie that day.

"*Gruuuuzik!*" Bonzo grunted as he carried his trumpet to music club.

Thanks to Zed, it was a great time to be a zombie. Even human kids were wearing Zed's signature Z on their clothes and homemade fake Z-Bands.

"Zombie chic," Zed praised them. "I like it! Looking good, guys!"

Human kids were not just dressing like zombies. For the first time in Seabrook history, they were rocking their own styles and looking less like pastel-colored clones.

Zed grinned to himself as he signed another autograph. Progress was all around at Seabrook High. And it was about time!

As he walked to his locker, he saw Addison and gave her a smile.

There was nothing Addison wanted more than to smile back, but with Bucky at her side, how could she? All she could do was ignore Zed and walk away.

Zed sighed as he opened his locker door. An explosion of silver confetti poured out, followed by a handwritten note. Who was it from?

Zed read it to himself: "Cheering for you on the inside. . . . XO Addison."

Over the moon, Zed read the note three times. But when he turned around to thank Addison, he saw her being dragged away by the Aceys.

Carefully, Zed placed Addison's note in his locker. Zombies on the football team, in the cafeteria, and in human classrooms were an awesome start. So were zombie fashions. But because of kids like Bucky and the Aceys, zombies still had a long way to go.

CHAPTER 16

Weeks later, Zed was still racking up amazing victories on the football field.

"Who's the best principal ever?" Principal Lee's voice exclaimed over the PA system. "Yeah, that's right—five wins in a row for the football team!"

Bucky stopped practicing in the gym to scowl at the announcement.

"It's a catastrophe," Bucky groaned. He turned to a poster of himself from happier, pre-zombie times and caressed it lovingly. "Oh, the life we lived."

Bree was having too much fun to notice the

announcement. Flipping on the trampoline, she shouted, "I feel so free! One day, I'll stick a hip-hop-double-tuck-Lindy!"

Addison wished she could feel as free as Bree. Ever since being told to ignore Zed, all she felt was a dark cloud hanging over her head every day. Her mood hardly lifted when she saw the Aceys walking over. Draped over Stacey's arm was a shiny, blinged-out jacket.

"Your cheer jacket arrived," Stacey said.

But when she held it up, Addison frowned. There had to be a mistake.

"Umm . . . it says Casey," Addison pointed out.

Tracey beamed as he nodded his head. "Now you can be an Acey too!" he declared. "Stacey, Lacey, Tracey—and Casey!"

Addison shook her head. "I can't change my name."

"I did," Lacey said. "My real name is Jenny."

Addison stared at Lacey . . . uh, Jenny. Wait . . . seriously?

"Jenny is a good name," Addison insisted. "As is Addison. Hey, just spitballing here, but why don't we keep our names?"

Not giving it a thought, Lacey chirped, "Come on, Casey."

Addison knew she was defeated, again. First the cheerleaders made her give up Zed. And now her own name!

But . . . whatever. Addison cracked a wooden smile as she slipped on the jacket. "Er . . . thanks," she murmured. As she caught a glimpse of herself in the mirror, she had to admit she looked pretty amazing. "Doesn't feel half bad," she told the Aceys. "And it's a really well-made cheer jacket."

Bree joined Addison at the mirror. She read the shiny embroidery on the jacket and wrinkled her nose. "Casey?" she asked. "So would I be . . . Bracey?"

The Aceys rolled their eyes at Bree. They clapped their hands in her face, then abruptly turned and walked off, calling, "Aceys, awayceys!"

Bree sighed as the Aceys twirled away. She turned to Addison, still at the mirror. "Rude," she whispered. "Do you believe those guys?"

Addison didn't answer Bree. Instead, she clapped her hands too, and twirled to join the other Aceys.

"Aceys!" Addison cheered. "Awayceys!"

Bree was shocked and hurt. "Addison," she called

after her. "Why are you acting like this?"

"Because this is what cheerleaders do!" she called back. Addison was about to follow the Aceys when something clicked. Maybe it was the cheer jacket having a kind of weird effect over her. Whatever it was, Addison knew she was turning into one of them—and that was so messed up!

"Oh, I'm so sorry, Bree! That was so jerky!" Addison said, walking back to her friend. "This isn't what cheerleaders do. This isn't who I am. I don't know who I am."

Bree smiled as the two friends hugged. Then Addison shrugged off the blinged-out bogus Casey jacket and let it drop to the floor.

Addison still didn't know who she truly was. She just knew for sure who she was not, and that was an Acey!

CHAPTER 17

"**D**eep fry me and dip me in cocktail sauce! Another win thanks to Zombie Zed!"

The announcer was excited, and so was the crowd, jumping to their feet and waving signs. Zed had scored another win for the Mighty Shrimp and for Seabrook High.

Zed grinned as his teammates carried him off the field on their shoulders. He had killed it again—thanks to his trusty Z-Band.

"*RRRrrragaz!*" Zed exclaimed. "Whoa!"

Realizing he was still zombied up, Zed quickly

swiped his Z-Band, returning himself to normal.

"Riiiiight on!" Zed shouted. Whew. That was close.

The crowd was still going wild as the announcer proclaimed, "The Mighty Shrimp have scampied their way to a perfect season. Homecoming game is next!"

Zed knew what a big deal the homecoming game was. But as long as his Z-Band delivered, so would he!

He looked across the field at Addison. She was surrounded by an upbeat cheer squad and happy fans. Addison looked anything but happy, but she did look surprised when Bonzo suddenly appeared at her side. What was up?

"Hey," Addison said.

"Zed-ski," Bonzo replied. He handed Addison an origami-style note folded to look like a bird. After a big Bonzo bear hug, he hurried off.

Curious, Addison unfolded the note and read it to herself: "Ready to break every rule in the book? Meet me at the barrier at 7 PM tonight. Zed."

Addison smiled. She knew she could get into huge trouble for secretly meeting a zombie, but she missed Zed and was tired of ignoring him.

"I'm in," Addison told herself.

Her spirits flew high as she folded the note back into a bird. She was going to meet a zombie boy tonight, and she wasn't freaked out at all.

That night, after the sun went down, Addison snuck out of her house. Carefully and quietly, she made her way to the concrete barrier separating Zombietown from the rest of Seabrook. She was just beginning to wonder whether meeting Zed was actually a good idea when she saw him.

"I'm here," Addison said in a shaky voice. "And I'm totally not freaked out at all."

"You're going to love this," Zed said.

Addison took a deep breath and grabbed Zed's hand. "Okay," she said. "Let's do this!"

Zed led the way as they entered what used to be the Seabrook Energy Plant. They stepped inside an old-timey freight elevator that creaked and groaned its way up.

"I missed you," Addison said. "So much."

"Me too," Zed said as he discreetly rubbed the area around his Z-Band.

The elevator inched up as Addison studied Zed. He looked paler than usual, and tired. "Hey, are you okay?" she asked. "You don't look so hot."

"Ouch," Zed chuckled.

"You know what I mean," Addison said.

Zed cared too much about Addison to hide the truth from her. Looking her straight in the eye, he said, "I have to mess with my Z-Band to win the games."

"Isn't that dangerous?" Addison asked.

"If I don't win, zombies will never be accepted," Zed explained. "Believe me, it's hard not being the real me. I hate it."

"I know how that feels," Addison sighed.

The elevator rumbled as it jerked to a stop.

"Are you ready for this?" Zed asked with a grin.

The door screeched open. As they stepped out, Addison gasped. They were inside a ramshackle old boiler room. But the only thing heating up was a full-blown zombie party!

Addison stared wide-eyed at the space decorated with repurposed junk. The electronics were retro, but the pulsating sounds were fresh, as zombies danced crazily to the beat. This party was totally lit!

"Are you serious?" Addison cried happily.

"It's a zombie mash," Zed explained. "A chance to get loose and be ourselves."

Addison was all for that. As they squeezed through the crowd, partiers welcomed them, some clapping

Zed on the back. Everyone was happy and ready for fun.

"This whole celebration is for you winning football games?" Addison shouted above the music.

"It's more than that," Zed said. "It's a win for all of us. And we really needed a win."

"You really support each other," Addison said approvingly.

She stopped to admire a mural on the wall. There was an image of a Z-Band surrounded by shapes that looked like hieroglyphics.

"It's Zombie tongue," Zed explained. "We have a rich language—twenty-three different words for 'brains.'"

Addison had only one word to describe the party— "magical." "I thought zombie parties would be dead and full of stiffs," she joked.

"Ha, ha, pretty clever," Zed said with a grin.

Addison felt on a roll with the zombie jokes. "So . . . do you like a girl with braaaaaains—"

"That is super offensive," Eliza's voice cut in.

Addison turned to Eliza. "Oh no," she said quickly. "I was joking. Sorry."

Refusing Addison's apology, Eliza angrily faced

Zed. "You brought Little Miss Cheer-Boots to our zombie mash? A human? Here?"

Before Zed could reply, a loud rumble grew from the far side of the room. "It's starting!"

Addison felt the crowd push past them. What was starting? She followed Zed and the others to a giant, tarnished boiler. Attached to it were pressure release valves. They were so big, a few zom-kids had to use all their strength to turn them.

As steam blasted throughout the room, Addison looked around for Zed. Where did he go?

"Zed?" Addison called. "Hello?"

She glanced up to see Bonzo on the balcony, rocking out in a homemade DJ booth.

"*Gruzik!*" Bonzo shouted.

On the other side of the room, Eliza worked the lights. Addison watched as the steam turned a vivid green. Onto a screen of steam Eliza projected a vintage zombie movie. The foot-dragging, flesh-rotting zombie was scary enough to make Addison flinch until a different zombie slipped in front of the flick. A very real and adorable zombie. Addison smiled. It was Zed!

The crowd went wild at the sight of their football

hero. But Zed wasn't up there to make a speech. He was there to sing and dance!

Bonzo cranked up the sound as Zed blew the place away with an original rap. The keyed up vibe was contagious as a group of zombie dancers moved rhythmically behind Zed. Even Eliza joined in, rapping and challenging Addison to a dance-off!

Addison had a blast dancing and rapping with her new zombie friends. She had never felt so free in her life, or so proud of Zed. He wasn't just the man on the football field—he was the man on the dance floor!

Just when things couldn't get cooler, a zombie mosh pit formed underneath Addison and Zed. Addison was too busy feeling the love to notice Zed rubbing his blistered wrist. Maxing out his Z-Band was beginning to catch up with him.

The song ended and everyone cheered. As the steam cleared Addison and Eliza looked around for Zed.

"Zed?" Addison called. When he didn't answer, she turned to Eliza. "Where did he go?"

CHAPTER 18

Addison looked all over the boiler room. When she couldn't find Zed, she made her way to another room in the back of the plant. She didn't find Zed, but she did discover the most incredible forest of blinking lights. Exposed light bulbs stuck out of vertical poles like a forest of lights. It was a zombie light-garden! And standing among the lights was a little girl waving pom-poms made from shredded newspaper.

The girl didn't see Addison as she continued her cheer: "I'm crazy! I'm cute! A zombie, to boot! I'm rockin'! I smile! Zombies aren't vile!"

Addison recognized the girl from that horrible initiation night in Zombietown. Stepping out of the shadows, she let herself be seen.

When the girl noticed Addison, she hid her pom-poms behind her back. "I wasn't doing anything," she blurted. "Certainly not cheering. Please don't tell anyone."

Addison smiled warmly. "That was some good cheering," she said. "You're Zed's sister, right?"

Zoey recognized Addison too, from the Mighty Shrimp games.

"I'm Zoey, and you're Addison," she said. "Cheering makes me happy."

"Me too," Addison agreed, "And seeing you rock it reminded me how great being a cheerleader can be. Thank you."

Addison pointed at Zoey's handmade pom-poms, now at her sides. "You are a great cheerleader, Zoey."

"Thanks," Zoey said. "But my pet, Zander, doesn't seem so impressed."

Zander? Addison looked to see where Zoey was pointing. Positioned to watch Zoey's cheerleading routine was a stuffed dog.

"He's great," Addison said. "But you're old enough

for a real pet. Wouldn't that be awesome?"

Eliza stormed into the room, surprising Addison. "Stop teasing her, Addison," she said. "You know they don't allow zombies to have pets."

"I didn't know," Addison admitted. "I'm still learning that zombies aren't what I was taught."

Addison nodded at Eliza and said, "I mean, look at you. You're smart, cool, pretty—"

"You think I'm pretty?" Eliza cut in.

"Of course you are," Addison insisted.

"There you are!" Zed's voice called out.

Addison was happy to see Zed entering the back room. He looked happy to see Addison and Eliza, but not his little sister.

"Zoey, what are you doing here?" Zed asked.

"Snuck out again," Zoey replied with a shrug.

"Again?" Zed groaned. "Zoey—"

"Come on, Zed?" Zoey said, lifting an eyebrow. "Whozzah good boy?"

Zed rolled his eyes. Not the big-brother-as-puppy routine again! But just like a puppy, Zed was loyal. He dropped to all fours and said, "Me."

Zoey giggled, petting Zed's head. Addison smiled too at Zed's puppy antics. Watching him play along with his little sister made her like him even more.

"I'll walk you home, Zoey," Eliza told her. "Zed has to make sure Addison makes it out of here."

"We should hang out, Eliza," Addison said. "And by the way, I really like your boots."

"Thanks!" Eliza said, flattered. "They're orthopedic. I've got a draggy-foot thing going on."

As Zoey collected Zander and her pom-poms, Eliza whispered to Zed, "Addison's cool."

"For a human, right?" Zed teased.

"No, she's just cool," Eliza said. She turned to Addison and added, "You guys look good together."

"We do, don't we?" Addison said with a sideways glance at Zed. Their two worlds really were beginning to unite. Maybe having a zombie boyfriend wasn't such a crazy idea after all.

Maybe . . . someday.

Alone in the back room, Zed and Addison gazed into each other's eyes. Before she could stop it, Addison felt a lock of her silvery hair drop out from beneath her wig. She tried to cover it with her hand, but it was too late. Zed had already noticed.

"It's beautiful," Zed said, putting his hand over Addison's. "*You're* beautiful."

Just then, shouts, screams, and chaos arose from the boiler room. Before Addison and Zed could wonder what was up, the door crashed open. In swarmed the Zombie Patrol, flashlights blazing.

"Zombies, show yourself!" a patrol officer barked. "You are out past curfew!"

Zed darted off to hide behind a pile of rubble. Addison rushed to fix her wig just as the blinding light hit her face.

The patrol officer's own face softened when he realized Addison was human. And not just any human, but the daughter of the chief Zombie Patrol officer.

"What are you doing here, Addison?" he asked. "This is a hotbed for zombie activity and not safe for humans. Let's get you home."

Addison tried not to look back at Zed's hiding place as she followed the officer out. Explaining to her parents that she was at a zombie party wouldn't be easy, but it was still easier than the zombies had it in Seabrook.

Perhaps "someday" wouldn't be as soon as she thought.

CHAPTER 19

"**Y**ou snuck out?" Missy cried. "Addison!"

"You know how dangerous it is out there," Dale said.

Addison stood grim-faced as she listened to her parents. The Zombie Patrol officer hadn't mentioned she was at a zombie party, and Addison was not about to volunteer that information!

"This town is full of monstrous zombies!" Missy said. "What were you up to?"

There it was—the Z word. So Addison thought fast. "I—I—I was out with a boy," she blurted.

"Oh boy," Dale muttered.

"Who is this boy?" Missy asked.

Addison's lips were zipped. No way could she tell her parents about Zed.

"You are not cheering," Missy stated firmly. "And no cheer championship until we meet this boy."

Addison stared at her mom. Whaaaaat? No cheering? Wasn't that a bit harsh?

"We need to meet this boy, Addison," Dale agreed. "Or you'll never cheer again."

Her parents' demands left Addison speechless. How could she not compete in the cheer championship? Then again, how could she introduce her parents to Zed?

Addison's magical night had turned into a nightmare. But night slowly turned to day, and things at school were getting back to normal. Everything except Zed's Z-Band. . . .

"I'm all for you trampling the system and the opposing team," Eliza told Zed. "But you have to stop messing with your Z-Band. It's not safe."

As Zed pulled books from his locker, he knew Eliza was right. But they had both escaped the Zombie Patrol the night before, so what was one more risk?

"I just have one more game to get through," Zed promised.

Eliza knew it was the most important game—the homecoming game. She tilted her head at Zed and asked, "Then no more hacking your Z-Band?"

"Totally!" Zed promised.

It was his and Eliza's biggest secret. But after they shut their lockers and headed for their classes, it was a secret no more. That was because three locker doors down, the Aceys had heard everything loud and clear!

"Zed's cheating!" Tracey declared.

Lacey's eyes flashed. "He's messing with his—"

"Z-Band!" Stacey cut in.

The Aceys slammed their locker doors and were off. Wickedly awesome news such as this was meant to be shared—with Bucky!

Zed didn't notice the Aceys zipping by him as he headed for the staircase. From the bottom of the stairs, he saw Addison on the second level. Calling her name, Zed raced up to meet her.

"Last night, I wanted to help when the Zombie Patrol arrived," Zed said breathlessly, "But—"

"Zed, it's not your fault," Addison told him. "I understand. The big problem is that my parents won't let me cheer until they meet you."

Zed stared at Addison. Her parents wanted to meet him? Zombies really were coming a long way!

"Great," Zed said. "I'll win them over with my quick wit and charming smile!"

"Not great," Addison sighed. "They don't know you're a zombie."

"And they hate zombies," Zed added.

"Yes," Addison admitted. "I'm sorry."

"I'm sorry for making things difficult for you," Zed said gently.

"You did nothing wrong. You're just being yourself," Addison insisted. "And you're great!"

Addison cast her eyes down as she gave it a thought. "If my family can't accept zombies, then maybe I don't want to be a cheerleader anymore."

Zed couldn't believe what he had just heard. No way would he let Addison give up the most important thing in her life because of him.

"But you love cheerleading," Zed said. "It's what makes you—you."

Addison thought that was sweet, although she didn't know who she really was lately.

"I'll meet your parents," Zed promised with a

smile. "We'll get through this."

Addison was touched by Zed's offer. If only he knew what her parents were like!

"I wish I could just flip a switch and change everything," Addison said. "But I can't."

Zed's eyes followed Addison as she walked away. Flip a switch, yeah, if it was only that easy.

Hey, wait a minute. . . . Maybe it was! Zed glanced down at his Z-Band. Then, like a zombie rocket, he shot off.

CHAPTER 20

Bucky opened the door and entered the empty cheer lounge. He sank to his knees before the display of cheerleading trophies, turned his eyes upward, and cried out to the heavens.

"Cheer spirits, glory to all that is Firecracker and Sis-Boom-Bah. Send me a sign so my perfectly toned body can stop zombies from stealing our spotlight."

From the corner of his eye, he caught a Go Bucky sign waving outside the window. Had the cheer spirits heard his prayer? Stacey, Lacey, and Tracey rushed into the cheer lounge.

"We know how to stop Zed!" Tracey declared.

"He's been hacking his Z-Band!" Lacey exclaimed.

"It's all about Eliza!" Stacey sneered. "And she's using her computer to do it."

Bucky froze in his tracks. Zed hacking his Z-Band? Eliza? Perhaps the cheer spirits had been looking out for him after all!

"Sis. Boom. Bah," Bucky said with a sly smile. The cheerleaders wasted no time scheming the zombies' demise.

But after school, up in his room, Zed had important work too, and it wasn't exactly homework. . . .

"Eliza said not to swipe right," Zed told himself, his hand poised over his Z-Band. "This is going to hurt. But no risk, no reward."

꿍꿍ꑶ ꇥꓻꇘ ꙮꓷ

Over in Seabrook, Addison was about to take a risk of her own. Knowing it wouldn't be easy, she called her parents over for a talk.

"I can't do this anymore," Addison declared. "There's something you need to know about this boy."

Dale smiled. "Now we're getting somewhere!"

"Right," Addison said, taking a deep breath. "Okay, fine. He's a—"

DING-DONG!

Missy smiled as she headed for the door. "He's here!" she said cheerily.

Addison froze. Zed? Here? Now? Her parents couldn't see him before she broke the news!

"Wait!" Addison blurted. "Don't open it!"

"Don't be ridiculous," Dale chuckled.

Her stomach in knots, Addison followed her parents to the door. "Fine. Open it," she said, "Yes, my date for the homecoming game is—"

Missy flung the door open. "Handsome!" she said with a smile.

Handsome? Addison peered out from behind her mom. Standing on the front porch was Zed, but a totally different Zed. Gone was his shock of green hair. Gone were his pallid white skin and red-rimmed eyes.

Addison couldn't help but stare. He looked . . . human!

"Dashing," Dale said, getting a good look at Zed.

Zed flashed a debonair grin as he handed Missy a bouquet of fresh flowers.

"Thank you. They're beautiful," Missy gushed.

"So how do you know my daughter?" Dale asked, getting right down to business.

Zed beamed at Addison. "She's a cheerleader, and I'm on the football team."

"No, really?" Dale asked.

"Really," Zed confirmed.

Dale puffed out his chest. "Well, you know, I used to play a little ball myself."

"No, really?" Zed asked.

"Really," Dale replied. "I was fullback."

"Get out!" Zed exclaimed. "I'm a fullback!"

"Let's do it!" Dale said excitedly.

Still shocked, Addison watched as Zed and her dad broke into the Mighty Shrimp shout. . . .

"Let's go, Mighty Shrimp! Break! On five!"

Just like teammates, Zed and Dale traded a high five. Addison had seen enough.

"Okay," Addison said, squeezing past her parents. "We're off to homecoming."

"Nice to meet you," Zed told Missy and Dale.

"He's a nice boy," Missy whispered to her daughter.

"Very nice, Addison," Dale agreed. "Where did you dig him up?"

Addison stared at her dad. He didn't just say that, did he? "See you at the game!" she blurted.

Her parents waving from the porch, Addison hurried to lead the new human-looking Zed away!

"How did you—?" Addison started to ask.

"I adjusted my Z-Band," Zed explained matter-of-factly. "I can feel the energy coursing through my bones. It's awesome."

Addison still couldn't believe it was happening, but she finally understood. Zed had transformed himself into a human for her!

"We still have some time before the game," Zed said. "And I owe you a real date."

"A date?" Addison repeated.

Back at school, the Aceys invited Eliza to join them on a spa date.

Eliza had been alone in the cafeteria doing her homework when the Aceys breezed in with smiles and a promise for a makeover.

"We've been wrong about zombies this whole time," Lacey admitted.

"With some concealer, blush, contouring, highlights, and a little bit of hair dye," Tracey admitted, "you could look cute."

"And when's the last time you pampered yourself?" Lacey asked.

Eliza shook her head. Hot-cocoa foot soaks and seaweed facials were not this zom-girl's idea of an awesome time. Especially with the Aceys!

"Uh, giggling over makeup and polishing each other's toenails?" Eliza said. "No sale."

Tracey and Lacey traded looks. Okay, plan A didn't work. There was still plan B.

"You like computers, right?" Lacey asked Eliza. "My mom just set up a whole VR room."

Eliza looked up from her books at Lacey. Now they were talking.

"Really?" Eliza asked. "I mean, I don't want to discriminate against humans, so in a way, it would be wrong for me not to take you up on your offer to play the latest VR games. Okay. I'm in."

Eliza was so excited that she didn't notice Stacey creeping up behind her. Or stealing her computer from her backpack!

Lacey waited until Stacey slipped out of the cafeteria with Eliza's computer. "On second thought," she told Eliza, "maybe not."

Eliza watched, bewildered, as the two giggling Aceys walked away. What was up with that?

CHAPTER 21

"**U**gh, I can't access it," Lacey complained. "There's a firewall on Eliza's computer."

Bucky, Stacey, and Tracey watched over Lacey's shoulder as she tried to hack Eliza's files.

"But we're so close," Bucky said impatiently.

Lacey typed furiously. She entered random codes until suddenly—"OMG! I can't believe it!" she cried. "The software's corrupted. We're in!"

Bucky and the Aceys cackled in unison. They were in. And if everything worked out as secretly planned, Zed—and all zombies—would be out!

While Bucky and the Aceys huddled over Eliza's computer, another cheerleader had a date with a zombie. Or someone who used to be one.

Zed smiled as he opened the door to the frozen yogurt shop. "Like I said, a proper date."

Addison walked inside. Still holding the door, Zed winced in pain. He leaned against the wall and rubbed his arm near his Z-Band.

"Are you okay?" Addison asked, peering around the door.

Zed pulled it together fast. "Yeah," he said. "Perfectly fine. Eliza was wrong. Nothing bad happened."

He followed Addison into the frozen yogurt shop, ignoring the sign on the door reading NO ZOMBIES.

Zombie? Where? Who? Not him—thanks to his Z-Band!

Zed and Addison sat at a table, where they checked out the menu. The flavors of the day were the same as they were every day: vanilla, vanilla, double vanilla, and vanilla!

"A wide variety," Zed joked.

"Of vanilla," Addison sighed. "This is Seabrook."

"Vanilla works," Zed decided. He put down his menu and glanced around. "I always wanted to come here. And now here I am with you, on a date."

Addison was happy to be on a date with Zed too. And he did make a super-adorable human. But something wasn't right.

"You're forced to be someone you're not, Zed," Addison told him. "Here and on the football field."

"So? You wear a wig to fit in," Zed pointed out. "Why can't I do the same thing with my Z-Band? Why is that so bad?"

"Because it's not right," Addison said. "We're changing ourselves when what needs to change is everybody else."

Deep down inside, Zed knew Addison was right. But there wasn't enough time to change the world when the homecoming game was later that day.

Besides, he might have been transformed from zombie to human, but he was still an optimist!

"Addison, we're making it work," Zed said with confidence. "I'll dial myself back to zombie mode and win the game. Everything is great!"

Addison hoped he was right.

CROW RAF CROW

After their date, he was still on her mind as she and

the other cheerleaders prepped for the game.

Through a thick haze of hair spray, glossed lips, blushed cheeks, and ponytails, Addison stood behind Bree, putting a bow in her hair.

"Take your pom-poms out there with you today, Bree," Addison told her.

"But I'm not a starter," Bree said.

"Who says?" Addison asked firmly. "It's time things changed around here."

Across the room, Bucky strutted before the mirror and grinned. No styling or spraying necessary. His hair was always perfect.

"Tonight everything changes," Bucky told himself. "Soon all anyone will care about is our squad winning the cheer championship."

CHAPTER 22

"**T**ime out! Time out!" Coach shouted.

The scoreboard clock stopped. Three seconds were left in the game, and Seabrook was down by five points.

"It's a whale of a game," the announcer piped up. "A nail-biter, as the Mighty Shrimp, down by five, call their final time out."

It didn't stop zombie fans in the stands from waving Go Zed signs and chanting his name.

The Mighty Shrimp players headed to the sidelines, where they surrounded Coach for a pep talk.

"Dare to dream, gentlemen," Coach told them. "We could win this. I could even keep my job. Dare to dream!"

"Let's go, Mighty Shrimp! Break! On five!" the players shouted.

As the players took the field, Principal Lee approached Coach. "People really love Zed," she said. "It's almost like he's one of us."

"He *is* one of us," Coach replied.

"You're right," Principal Lee agreed.

Zed felt the love from his fans. He also felt exhaustion as he slumped down on the bench. He raised his Z-Band to inspect his blistering wrist. The extreme transformation process was doing him in. But in the end, it would all be worth it.

"You okay?" a voice asked.

Zed looked up to see Addison. "Yeah, yeah. Almost there," he told her. "I do this and we win."

"I'll be cheering for you," Addison promised.

Zed watched Addison walk back to the field. He stood, put on his helmet, and left to join his team for the final stretch.

As Zed took to the field, Addison grabbed a megaphone. Turning toward the crowd, she began to shout, "This is our school and that is our team. Let's cheer 'em. Who's with me?"

The crowd began to roar. Addison stood alone as she shared the spirit. "Give me a ZOM, give me a BIE! What does that spell?"

"Zombie!" the crowd yelled, on their feet.

Addison smiled at the fired-up crowd until she felt Bucky grab her arm and spin her around.

"You're way too good a cheerleader to throw your life away," Bucky hissed.

"I'm cheering for a change, Bucky," Addison said.

Bucky shot Addison a warning look as she turned back to the stands. "Don't do it," he said.

"Come on, give me a ZOM!" Addison shouted.

"ZOM!" the crowd shouted back.

"Addison," Bucky said through gritted teeth.

"Give me a BIE," Addison cheered.

"BIE!" The crowd cheered too.

"Last chance," Bucky warned.

"What does that spell?" Addison asked.

"ZOMBIE!" the crowd boomed.

Bucky charged over to Addison like a raging bull. "You're off the squad, you freak!" he screamed at her.

Addison paid no attention to her cousin. Neither

did Bree as she joined in with her pom-poms.

"Go, zombies," Bree cheered. "Go, Zed!"

"You're off the squad too!" Bucky yelled at Bree.

Addison and Bree kept cheering for zombies, amping up the crowd. Zombie haters, like Addison's parents, were not amused. But Zevon, Bonzo, Eliza, and Zoey were tickled to death!

"Bet they're going to let us have pets soon!" Zoey said, bouncing in her seat. "I'm going to get a giraffe!"

She caught her dad's disapproving look. "Fine . . . a pony!"

A whistle blast told everyone the game was about to resume. Nail-biting resumed too, as the announcer reminded everyone what was at stake: "Fifty yards to go and three seconds on the clock. The Mighty Shrimp will need a jumbo-sized miracle to win this one."

Zed knew he had this. Glancing down at his Z-Band, he gave it a swipe. The word "Offline" appeared, causing his stomach to twist. Then an icon of a troll's face appeared.

"It's not working?" Zed gasped.

In a panic, he looked to Eliza in the stands and mouthed, "HEEEEEELPPPPP!"

CHAPTER 23

Eliza and Bonzo sprang to their feet, knowing Zed was in trouble. Eliza took a wild guess it had something to do with his Z-Band.

She glanced down at her own Z-Band. Her legs turned to jelly upon seeing the troll-face icon.

"Software's corrupted? How?" Eliza cried. She looked up at Zed pacing on the football field. "Ugh, Zed. What did you do?"

"Hagrazacked?" Bonzo asked. He checked out his Z-Band too. Another troll face!

"Yeah, we're totally being hacked," Eliza said.

But who was responsible? To find out, Eliza and Bonzo stormed down the bleachers. At the same time, underneath the bleachers, the Aceys crowded around Eliza's laptop. On the screen was a picture of Zed plus his Z-Band flashing OFFLINE. Nearby were the words "Stage Two Standby."

"Stage one is done," Lacey declared. She handed the laptop to Stacey and ran off.

The stadium was still fired up, cheering and waving Go Zed signs. Zed knew he was in deep trouble. Without a working Z-Band, how would he receive a surge of zombie-power? But when he saw Addison cheering on the sidelines, he felt another kind of power—confidence.

"I can still do this," Zed told himself. "Even as regular old me. I can do this."

The quarterback passed the ball. Zed worked his football smarts to stay on his feet. He juked an attacker, spun away from a defender, stiff-armed a cornerback, and after finding a hole, charged toward the end zone.

With his eyes on the goal line, Zed charged with the ball.

Five yards from the end zone, a swarm of opposing players moved to stop him—until Zed found himself smack at the bottom of a dog pile. Still holding the ball, Zed found an opening. The crowd went wild as Zed lurched his hand out from under the pile and held the ball over the goal line!

"I did it!" Zed exclaimed. "Yes! Touchdown!"

The crowd jumped to their feet, eager to hear the ref's call. Zed was still under a dog pile but felt on top of the world. Who needed a surge of zombie power from his Z-Band? Not him!

As the ref approached the heap of players, Stacey sat at Eliza's computer. This time, Eliza and Bonzo appeared on the screen along with graphics of their Z-Bands.

"Stage two, initiated!" Stacey declared pressing the key. With a satisfied nod, she handed the laptop to Tracey and rushed off.

The ref was about to make his call when Zed noticed his Z-Band flickering. As it began flashing red, so did Zed's eyes. With more zombie power than ever before, he burst from the pile of players, ripped off his helmet, and let out a mighty "ROOOOOOAAAARRRRR!"

The Z-Alert alarms blared as players and fans scattered in every direction away from Zed. They always knew he was a zombie, but this zombie was of the old-school brain-eating, face-ripping variety!

"Braaaaaains!" Zed howled.

Everyone stared horrified at their football hero, now a mutant monster. Meanwhile, underneath the bleachers, there was more damage about to be done. . . .

"Stage three," Tracey said cheerfully. "Initiate!" He pressed a key on Eliza's laptop. "This is soooo cool!"

Along the sidelines, Eliza and Bonzo ran toward Zed. Just as they were passing the cheerleaders, they froze.

Everyone watched as Eliza and Bonzo morphed into flesh-hungry, full-blown, hulking zombies!

"Arrrrrrrrrrrrgh!" Bonzo growled.

"Graaaaaaarrrrr!" Eliza snarled.

Bucky gleefully turned to all three Aceys. "Our plan is working!" he exclaimed. "I thought of everything!"

"Great," Lacey said. "So how do we stop that monster from eating our brains?"

Bucky gulped when he saw Zed roaring straight at them. Uh-oh. He'd thought of everything except that!

CHAPTER 24

With Zed charging full speed ahead, the Aceys ran in the other direction. They practically screeched to a stop when they saw Eliza and Bonzo coming at them too.

"Together we could take them," Lacey whispered.

"Totally," Stacey whispered before racing away.

Tracey shoved Lacey forward. "She's much tastier!" he said before racing off too.

Eliza and Bonzo flashed rotting zombie teeth at Lacey. "Arrrrgggh!"

Chaos erupted on the football field as Bucky

searched for an escape. He scurried underneath the bleachers, hearing growls behind him. Thinking he was being chased, Bucky ran faster until Zed stepped out of the shadows. Like a ferocious grizzly bear, he staggered forward, swiping at Bucky.

Bucky tripped and fell to the ground. He was frozen with fear as Zed raised his powerful arm. But just as Zed was about to strike, he lurched back and dropped to his knees.

Zed was trying with all his might to fight off the monstrous urge. His cold, hard gaze softened when he saw Addison run over.

Addison knelt beside Zed and said softly, "It's going to be okay. Take my hand and we'll get you some help."

Zed could hardly lift his head but turned pleading eyes toward Addison. He was about to take her hand when Dale and two Zombie Patrol officers stormed over. Too exhausted to fight back, Zed let them drag him away.

"Threat neutralized," one officer said into his walkie-talkie. "We're bringing them in."

"No!" Addison shouted to her father. "Leave him alone!"

"Addison, stay back," Dale warned.

Shouts and boos rose from the crowd as the zombies were escorted to the sidelines. Their own Z-Bands had been replaced with heavy-duty industrial ones.

Zevon, Dale, Missy, and Principal Lee watched the zombies being readied for transport. All three would be taken to zombie containment.

"Stop!" Addison pleaded. "They're my friends."

"We told you, Addison," Dale said. "Zombies are not safe. Give them an inch—"

"And they'll bite your face off," Missy cut in.

Zevon couldn't believe what he was hearing. "Hey, that's my son you're talking about!" he snapped.

Dale and Missy turned away, but Principal Lee approached Zed's dad. "I suggest you move along, Mr. Necrodopolous," she said gently. "I'll make sure they treat him okay. I'm sorry."

"Zed!" Addison called. "Please."

Zed didn't want Addison anywhere near him. Not now.

"I'm sorry, Addison," Zed called softly. Hanging his head, he added, "Maybe they're right. Maybe we shouldn't be together."

"Don't say that!" Addison gasped.

Before Zed could say another word, he and his

friends were loaded into a patrol van and hauled away.

The Aceys watched in disbelief. Bucky too was stunned. Sure, he wanted the zombies off the football team, but this wasn't what he had in mind.

The crowd wasn't silent as they turned on the zombies. "Zombie freaks!" they yelled. "Monsters! We should have known!"

Hearing the ugly words was more than Addison could take. Enough was enough. She was speaking up!

"You did this to him!" Addison shouted to the stands. "You made him feel like he had to risk his life to belong because you couldn't deal with someone different. But you had no problem using him to win your stupid game!"

Addison wasn't finished. Planting her feet firmly, she took hold of her wig and pulled it off.

Those who saw Addison's silver head of hair whispered and called her a freak too. But Addison didn't care. For the first time in her life, she felt proud of what made her different. And for the first time ever, she felt free!

CHAPTER 25

The Zombie Containment officer slid the van door open with a bang. Zed, Eliza, and Bonzo stepped out and joined their parents. After being contained in Seabrook for hours, they were finally back in Zombietown.

Zed was happy to be home but still felt bad about the zombie meltdown.

Looking at his freshly updated Z-Band, Zed smiled. All zombies would be getting their Z-Bands updated. The new ones couldn't be tweaked or hacked.

"Sweet! " Zed told Eliza. "They have Wi-Fi now!"

Eliza glowered back at him. It was too soon to make jokes. After all, it was their dumb Z-Bands that had gotten them in trouble in the first place.

As their parents walked ahead, Eliza gritted her teeth in anger. "Cheerleaders stole my computer and sabotaged everything, and yet zombies get blamed. It was stupid to think humans were going to change."

Zed had seen Eliza mad before, but never this mad.

"We tried doing it the nice way," Eliza went on. "It's time we do it my way. A zombie uprising. Force them to make us equal, or we tear it all down!"

"Eliza," Zed said. "Change takes time."

"I've been waiting my whole life," Eliza muttered. "I'm sick of waiting."

Zed watched Eliza and Bonzo head off with their parents. Zed's dad walked over and put an arm around his shoulders.

"You could have died adjusting your Z-Band," Zevon said gently. "You don't have to change who you are, Son. I love who you are."

"Yeah, but the humans don't," Zed sighed.

The next morning, the weather was as gloomy as the mood at Seabrook High. After the zombie meltdown at the homecoming game, it was open season for anyone who was different. Starting with the cheer squad . . .

"I've been watching you," Bucky snapped at the cheerleaders lined up against the wall. "And I know who the zombie sympathizers are!"

Addison had already been banished from the squad for her zombie support. But with the cheer championship just hours away, Bucky saw an opportunity. He was going to purge the squad of more zombie lovers!

"I see you!" Bucky said pointing to a cheerleader. "I see you, traitor!"

Bucky walked along the line of cheerleaders, picking them out one by one. "Zombie flair—you're out! You cheered for zombies with Addison—gone!"

"Bucky," Lacey said carefully. "What are you doing?"

In no time, Bucky was in Lacey's face. "Don't doubt me! We are cheerleaders," he snapped at her. "We are flawless. And that is why we will be perfect at the cheer championship tonight."

Bucky whirled around to the others. "So we are going to start at the beginning and go over our routine again. Over. And. Over. Get in position!"

As the cheerleaders took their places, the Aceys traded worried looks. Was Bucky losing it?

𝕮𝕽𝕰𝕻 𝕷𝕬𝕱 𝕮𝕽𝕰𝕻

There was even less cheer down in the basement, where zombies cleaned out their desks and packed their belongings. They were all being sent back to the zombies-only school.

Eliza hadn't shown up that morning, so Zed and Bonzo cleaned out her desk. In the middle of sorting out Eliza's papers, something caught Bonzo's eye. *"Eliza-ka zagrazazaboage!"* he exclaimed.

"Eliza's going to sabotage something?" Zed translated, before realizing what Bonzo said. "What?"

Bonzo waved handfuls of paper to imitate the cheerleaders' pom-poms. *"Chargzeer agrazoff!"*

Zed took the papers to see for himself. On one sheet was a hand-drawn control board and notes that read, "Main lighting console short circuit at 120 amps. Patch through to sound system."

Zed stared down at the plans. He looked up at Bonzo, his heart pounding. "Eliza's going to sabotage the cheer championship!"

122

CHAPTER 26

"It's been a tremendous day here at the regional cheer championship!"

The announcer wasn't kidding! The stands at the theater were packed with fans eager to support their home cheer squads. Performing a stunningly electric routine at that time were the Eastbay Eels.

"Only days after the first zombie incident in decades," the second announcer chimed in, "security has assured us we are safe to proceed."

The Eels sizzled as fans waved foam fingers and banners, cheering for the Eastbay squad as Bucky and the Aceys watched from the sidelines.

"Stay loose," Bucky said. "We're next."

Tracey heaved a sigh. "How's this going to work?"

"We're not even half a team!" Stacey complained.

Bucky frowned. He'd had no choice but to eliminate those zombie-loving traitors, even if they did make up most of their squad. "We're going to crush this," he insisted. "I can feel it in my gut!"

He also felt something he refused to admit: worry.

At the same time, Eastbay fans were on their feet for the Eels. But not everyone had spirit that afternoon. Way, way up in the stands, Addison and Bree watched the competition with sad eyes and aching hearts.

"I always dreamed of cheering here," Bree told Addison. "Soaring through the air as the crowd roared. Flying higher than anyone's ever flown." She shook her head as she slumped forward. "It was a stupid dream."

Tossing her silvery hair, Addison placed a reassuring arm around Bree. "You will fly," she promised. "Someday. As soon as this town gets over itself."

Addison gazed down the bleachers where her parents sat. Missy was glancing back at Addison disapprovingly. Addison knew what that was all about.

"I thought your parents didn't want you in public with your real hair," Bree said.

"They don't," Addison replied. "But they can't make me hide anymore." Steeling herself, Addison sat up straighter. "I'm not leaving this seat. No way. My dad's whole patrol couldn't get me out of this seat!"

Addison was about to turn her attention back to the competition when she spotted Zed and Bonzo. The two friends were flitting underneath the bleachers. But why? For what?

"It's Zed!" Addison said, bolting up. "I'm going to leave my seat."

It was a long walk from the top of the bleachers to the bottom. But Addison had to find out what was going on.

At the same time, Zed and Bonzo were walking up to Eliza. She and the zombie dancers from the mash had opened the theater's electrical box. They were in the middle of installing a tangle of cables and an old volt regulator.

"You can't do this, Eliza," Zed said.

"Do what?" Eliza asked coolly. "Enjoy the cheer

championship with my fellow zombies?"

"*Zagrazaboage!*" Bonzo accused.

"Sabotage? I'd never!" Eliza stated. She caught Zed's and Bonzo's doubtful looks and added, "Okay . . . maybe just a little sabotage."

"Ruining the cheer championship will only prove their worst fears—that zombies are monsters!" Zed exclaimed.

"They think that anyway," a voice said.

Zed and the zom-kids turned to see Addison. She seemed surprisingly calm.

"At least you have the guts to stand up for yourself," Addison told the zombies. "I say do it!"

"You're not changing my mind, Addison," Eliza snapped. "Wait. . . . You agree with me?"

Eliza slowly smiled, then said, "I like this girl!"

But Zed wasn't smiling, and neither was Bonzo.

"Sabotage isn't the zombie way," Zed said. "It's not who we are."

Work on the electrical box stopped as everyone listened to Zed. "I messed up, Addison," he said. "I wanted to play football so badly, and when I wasn't given a real chance, I changed who I was. But I'm not doing that anymore. I'm not a monster—I'm a zombie!" He moved closer to Addison, gazing into her eyes. "And you're a cheerleader. You can't change the world through sabotage. You change it through cheer. By bringing people together and bringing out their best!"

Moved by his words—and cute looks—Addison stepped closer to Zed. They were about to exchange a kiss when Eliza leaned in.

"So . . . no sabotage?" Eliza asked.

"No sabotage, Eliza," Addison said before smiling at Zed. "That's not who I am."

The zombie dancers turned away from the electrical box just as Bree dashed over. "Seabrook's up next!"

The Eels were performing their big finish when Addison, Zed, Eliza, Bonzo, Bree, and the zombie dancers hurried to watch.

"What a performance!" the first announcer boomed. "Squeals of appeal as the Eels finish with zeal!"

The Eels scored big. Everyone knew the Mighty Shrimp would have to bring it to hold on to their champion title.

"Put your hands together for our defending champions," the announcer boomed, "a team that needs no introduction!"

"But since we're doing it anyway," the other announcer said, "here are the almighty, outta-sighty Seabrook Shrimp that are mighty!"

Seabrook fans jumped up as Bucky backflipped into the theater to blazing fanfare. Landing on his feet, he blew the roof off with his famous blinding smile and signature pose.

Following Bucky were the Aceys and the rest of the squad—just a smattering of cheerleaders.

"That's a much slimmed-down squad," the first announcer noticed.

"A little too slim," the other agreed.

Ignoring the confused murmurs in the stands, the Mighty Shrimp built a pyramid. The lopsided formation toppled back and forth before crumbling to the ground.

Addison and Bree traded "ouch" looks. That was going to be a big deduction!

"Mighty Shrimp are mighty bad!" a heckler shouted.

Bucky cocked his ear to the stands. "What is that sound?" he asked.

"They're booing us," Lacey said.

"Losers!" another fan yelled. "What a freak show!"

Losers? Freaks? Bucky clutched his perfectly ripped chest in horror. Their team had never gotten such a reception before. What had he done by eliminating half of the squad? What was he thinking?

Suddenly, the squad's music cut out.

"There seems to be some technical difficulty with Seabrook's audio track," the first announcer reported.

While the audio tech tried to figure out the problem, angry voices filled the theater. First their pathetic pyramid and now their music. How bad could the Mighty Shrimp be?

Zed, Addison, Bonzo, Bree, and Eliza sat through the awkward silence until a tiny voice rose from the crowd: "Let's go, Seabrook. Cheer!"

The crowd stared in awe as a little zombie girl faced the stands. No one could see the plug to the audio system lying on the ground next to her feet. All they could see was a smiling zombie girl waving newspaper pom-poms as she happily cheered.

"Roll it, shake it. Victory—let's take it!"

Addison smiled too. Way to go, Zoey!

CHAPTER 27

"**G**-O, go!" Zoey went on. "Go, Shrimp, go!"

Bucky winced as he watched the kid-zombie cheerleader. He didn't know what was worse: being heckled—or her!

"You can do it—yes you can," Zoey cheered. "Bucky, Bucky, you're the man!"

"But . . . she's a zombie," Bucky said, bewildered. "Why is she cheering for me?"

"What is she doing?" Bree asked from the sidelines.

"She's changing things," Addison said excitedly, "by cheering."

Eliza frowned, pointing at Zoey. "This isn't how

things change," she said. "Not just one person standing with pom-poms!"

"You're right," Addison agreed. "It's going to take more than one person."

With that in mind, Addison turned to her friends, human and zombie. "It's going to take all of us," she told them. "Together, we can change this town. Together, we can save it!"

"Like they'll ever see us as normal," Eliza scoffed.

"They won't," Zed said, "because we're not normal."

"And they need to see that," Addison added. "Zombies celebrate their differences, so let's go out there and celebrate—cheer-championship style!"

Zed turned to Eliza and the zombie dancers. "You guys in?" he asked.

Eliza looked over at Zoey. If that little kid could put herself out there, what was her excuse?

"This is our revolution," Eliza declared. Then, under her breath, she muttered, "But did it have to be cheer? Ugh."

Zoey was still waving her pom-poms when a fan shouted, "Sit down, you zombie freak!"

Addison's blood boiled at the mean jeer. That did it. She marched in front of the stands, faced the

131

crowd along with Zoey, and began to cheer.

"That's okay, that's all right! C'mon, Seabrook—fight, fight, fight!"

Addison took Zoey's hand in hers. More jeers rose from the stands.

"Down in front, you white-haired weirdo!" a fan heckled.

"Yeah, zip it, freaks!" another shouted.

Addison threw back her shoulders and shouted back. "That's right—we're freaks. But all of us are different, and what makes us different is what makes us mighty!"

Zed was also fed up with the jeering and booing. He marched over to Addison and Zoey, facing the angry crowd.

"I'm a zombie," Zed declared. "And proud!"

"I'm different too!" Bree shouted proudly. "I'm left-handed!"

Addison's message was contagious as more and more humans declared what made them unique. A football lineman preferred chocolate ice cream to vanilla. The coach wanted to dance like no one was watching. Lacey really did want to be called Jenny . . . sometimes.

"Enough with the pastels!" the announcer shouted into the mike. "I want to wear leather and leopard-print pants!"

It wasn't long before the jeers of the hecklers were drowned out by the cheers of the Seabrook students. "Let's go, Seabrook!"

"What a feel-good moment we have here," the first announcer said. "But even if Seabrook manages to get their act together, it looks like the Mighty Shrimp's dynasty is about to come to an end."

Zed, Addison, and Eliza glanced over at Bucky. His famously perfect face wore a hangdog look as he stood alone.

"Bucky, things can change," Zed told him.

"I don't want change," Bucky muttered. "Change is what ruined everything."

"It's not over yet," Addison said. "We can still do this."

"Change is happening, Bucky," Eliza said. "Zombies are not going away. You can either fight us and lose or you can be a part of it."

Bucky looked at the line of humans and zombies together. Eliza was right. Change was happening, but for him, things were changing too fast.

"I—I can't," Bucky stammered. He pulled out his cheer whistle, handed it to Addison, and stormed off.

Zed wasted no time. He led the cheerleaders and zombie dancers in a team hand-stack. "Let's let our freak flags fly!" he exclaimed.

Addison smiled at the new and improved Mighty Shrimp cheer squad. "Okay," she said, "here's the plan."

CHAPTER 28

"The Seabrook Mighty Shrimp are back on the floor," the first announcer told the crowd, "and the technical difficulties have been sorted out!"

"They have to be perfect to even think of winning this," the second announcer added grimly.

The crowd waited silently in the darkened theater until BOOM! The lights flashed on to show cheerleaders and zombie dancers with their heads bowed down.

Just as everyone wondered about the weird formation, a blast of fired-up music kicked in. Zoey blew the whistle as humans and zombies came alive, all in a mixed cheer-and-zombie-dance routine.

"Zombies and cheerleaders are on the floor together!" the first announcer exclaimed. "You are watching history unfold!"

The crowd watched, spellbound, as humans and zombies combined their own special styles. They had come to play and were here to stay!

Addison's silvery hair lit up the stage as she whirled, twirled, flipped, and split. Nothing was going to get in her way anymore. While the Mighty Shrimp killed it on the dance floor, Bucky watched from the side. So did Zoey.

"They're good, right?" Zoey asked him.

"Yeah," Bucky said with a sigh. Who was he kidding? Those zom-kids had the moves and the grooves.

"Only thing they're missing," Zoey said, "is the best cheerleader I ever saw."

"That's true. I'm very good," Bucky said before quickly adding, "So are you."

"I know," Zoey said with a smile. She held out her hand, and Bucky took it. He then let the little zombie lead him to the front of the theater.

Bucky leaped onto the dance floor, breaking into a series of amazing moves and stunts.

With Bucky in the routine, the Mighty Shrimp were pumped to the max. When it was time for the big finish, all eyes turned to Addison. But the new head cheerleader didn't take her position. Instead, she grabbed Bree's hand.

The crowd watched from the edge of their seats as cheerleaders and zombies launched Bree high into the air. She flipped, tucked, and twisted flawlessly before landing softly in Bonzo's arms!

"Grazagraful, Breeska," Bonzo said with a grin.

"Awww," Bree said, smiling too. "That's the nicest thing anyone has ever said to me."

Bree finally knew what it was like to fly. And as the audience went wild, the Mighty Shrimp knew what it was like to totally crush it.

"Cheertastic!" both announcers shouted into their microphones.

The Mighty Shrimp cheer squad took a bow. Bucky stepped forward, then reached back for Addison and Zed, leading them in front of him.

Confetti exploded throughout the theater, celebrating Seabrook's awesome routine. Addison was super-happy as she turned to Zed. "Who would have thought a zombie and a cheerleader—"

"—could change the world," Zed cut in with a smile. "And get their happily ever after?"

"As they say in Zombie tongue," Addison said, *"Zjah garz argazah!"*

"Yeah," Zed said with a big smile. "I *garz argazah* you too."

They didn't win the cheer championship, but they did something even better: they brought everyone together. A few days later, for the first time ever, humans were invited to Zombietown to meet their zombie neighbors. Even Addison's parents showed up.

There were smokin' barbecues and thumpin' music, plus a hero's welcome for Zed, Seabrook's zombie football sensation. There was also a big surprise for Zoey. . . .

"A puppy!" Zoey cried when Addison handed her a real live dog. "My very own puppy!"

As Addison danced with Zed, her heart turned the perfect triple jump. Maybe they didn't have to wait for that "someday" when human and zombie worlds came together as one.

Maybe that "someday" was now!